Floating Souls

The Canal Murders

A Novel by

Mary H. Manhein

Floating Souls – The Canal Murders

Copyright © 2012 by Mary H. Manhein

Published by Margaret Media, Inc.
618 Mississippi Street
Donaldsonville, Louisiana 70346
www.margaretmedia.com
(225) 473-9319

First edition published 2012
Printed in the United States of America by
Sheridan Books, Chelsea, Michigan

ISBN: 9780982455197
Library of Congress Control Number: 2012938927

Book design by Irish Cabrini Creative
Cover art © Nicole deLaunay Harris

Acknowledgements

So many people have helped to bring this brief novel to the printed page. In terms of editing, I must begin by thanking David Madden and Malcolm Shuman. David and Malcolm have encouraged me from the beginning and I owe them a special gratitude. Along the way also, George Roupe, Mary Gehman, and Jason Moore have provided essential editing skills. I must also thank Ginny Listi, Missy Weaver, and Helen Bouzon for their reading and comments. Additionally, Nicole Harris' work on the cover art was outstanding.

Finally, I thank my husband Bill for all of his support throughout the process. He worked tirelessly to scan and rework the written copy of the manuscript years ago when the computer died.

Major Characters

Margaret (Maggie) Rose Andrepont
        Orleans Parish forensic anthropologist
Dr. Dan Farrington
        Orleans Parish coroner
Eduardo Phillipe Martusa
        Head of Antiquities in Rome and
        Maggie's college boyfriend
Lucas Evans
        Maggie's archaeology partner
Jimmy O'Malley
        Times Picayune ace reporter and
        Maggie's childhood friend
Moses Smith
        Maggie's gardener and all around helper who also
        worked for her parents in her childhood
Maura Stone
        Amateur archaeologist
Sidney Snyder
        Orleans Parish chief coroner's investigator
Dr. Patsy Browning
        Orleans Parish forensic pathologist
Rodney Durham
        local documentary producer
Brutus and Tango
        the most magnificent dog and cat, respectively

Floating Souls

The Canal Murders

Chapter 1

Maggie Andrepont prayed for just one uneventful night in New Orleans. The oppressive summer air pushed against her skin, sandwiching her between its humidity and the heat rising from the cracked and uneven sidewalk. She shivered as she watched the coroner's investigators slide the collapsed gurney carrying the body bag into the van parked against the curb. Two more women were dead in the city, at least what was left looked like two women. They had burned to a crisp in a French Quarter hotel bathtub. Most of their soft tissue was gone and their mouths seemed caught in the middle of a scream, their dental fillings reflecting brightly when police officers swept their flashlights back and forth across the darkened room. The smoke alarm in the room had a new battery, or the 150-year-old building would be a pile of rubble now. Candles and religious paraphernalia all around suggested Santeria, the religion du jour that had taken hold in some of the Caribbean islands and had made its way into the Crescent City off and on over the years. A cross between West African religions and

1

Christianity, it fit right in with some of the street freaks who populated the city. The residue of oil in the hotel tub and dead birds in the room supported Santeria, but something had gone wrong. The obvious clue was the chair pushed under the bathroom doorknob—from the outside. Someone who knew exactly what happened was now on the streets of New Orleans.

Next stop for the bodies would be the forensic anthropology laboratory at the parish morgue, Maggie's lab. But full-body x-rays and dental x-rays with the Nomad would wait until tomorrow. The Nomad, Maggie's new, portable x-ray gun, looked like the fake ray guns in the old Buck Rogers black and white television shows. One small problem. When Maggie helped to pick up what was left of the women, she could see inside their mouths. Identification for them might not be easy. Usually, dental identifications could be fairly uncomplicated, but you had to have an idea of who the victim might be and also find the right dentist. With tens of thousands of people missing across the country and no central database, the police needed a big clue in the hotel case. The investigators had an even greater problem with the women from the hotel. They had a lot of dental work but the materials for their fillings didn't look quite right. They might be from outside the U.S. They might never be identified.

Once home, Maggie filled her old claw-foot bathtub with tepid water and sank into its depths. Dragging the soggy washcloth filled with soap up and down her arms and legs, she tried to remove the odor of smoke and death from her pores. She willed the hotel case to the back of her mind. Death was a thriving business in New Orleans.

Falling into bed, she wanted nothing more than temporary relief from the memory of the women reduced to blackened caricatures of flesh and bone. She sank into a restless sleep. Her body rose. Her arms floated at shoulder height. Her legs disappeared. Cries for help from those below who were trapped in the debris of the burning and collapsed building propelled her toward them. The shrill of distant ambulances and the heat from a red sky jarred her into semi-consciousness. Finally, she realized that she had been dreaming and that the siren-like sounds were coming from the phone near her head. Waving her arm, she hit her antiquated receiver. The phone fell from its cradle and onto the floor. She leaned over to pick it up. The blood rushing to her head made her dizzy as she tried to focus on the caller. "Maggie, Maggie, are you there? There's another one in the canals. Can you come?"

"What? Dan? Is that you? Start over." Maggie blinked twice to clear her head. She glanced at the orange numbers on the clock. 5:45 a.m. She had been in bed for only three hours.

"There's a woman's body in the canal. Can you get here?"

"Where is she, Dan?"

"One of the feeder canals near City Park. Head that way and you'll see the lights."

"Be there as soon as I can." She hung up the phone, lying there for a moment or two longer, trying to shake the anxiety from her mind. The dream had come back. Why did she continue to have that nightmare where, helplessly, she watched from above as though she were dead, or worse still, in some kind of self-imposed purgatory? She had been raised Catholic but hadn't been to mass in years. Maybe it was time to go back. Maggie pushed Brutus, her Great Dane, off her tingling feet and left Tango, the cat, where he lay near her thigh. She hurried into the kitchen to heat water in the microwave.

The floors of her old building creaked and snapped as she went. The pipes at the kitchen sink vibrated when she turned on the cold-water tap to fill a cup for instant coffee. The taste would be little better than roof drippings from the rusted drain near the corner of her building, but she needed caffeine.

She walked to her chest of drawers on the other side of the bed, pacing her movements carefully as her lower back and left hip chimed in with their daily salutation. Something deep in their recesses was not happy. Fifteen years of bioarchaeology and forensic anthropology were taking their toll on her body. The result of climbing in and out of deep burial pits, whether archaeological or forensic, had forecast a shortening of what she had hoped would be a lifelong career.

Maggie's reflection in the mirror made her smile. Her hair was standing on end. Going to bed last night with it wet hadn't been such a good idea after all. Her auburn curls looked like corkscrews springing from her scalp in all directions. Wincing a little at the slight spreading and softening of an otherwise athletic figure, she gathered the longer strands of hair in one hand and fastened them with a clip. Once again, she vowed to cut her unruly curls to within an inch of her scalp. The idea seemed more reasonable with each new forensic case. Cutting it certainly would reduce her body's absorption area for the lingering hint of death only Maggie could detect. Sometimes the smell of putrefaction could be purged with a three-mile walk, a luxury she had not allowed herself in weeks.

She pulled jeans and a T-shirt from a drawer and then checked them for holes. They appeared to be in reasonably good shape. Slipping into what had become her uniform for field cases, she started thinking about the Orleans Parish coroner. For over twenty years, Dan

Farrington had been cataloging and investigating thousands of deaths in one of America's most crime-ridden cities. Of course, Maggie would help him. Surely he knew that. He and Maggie went way back, their history known only to a handful of people. He was among the few living who knew his old nickname for her. Knew it, and knew to keep it to himself.

A couple of weeks ago, Dan had publicly announced his bid for reelection. His new campaign signs were all over the city: "Coroner Farrington: always fair even when the weather's foul." Goofy, but sort of refreshing, right out of the 1950s. Part of it certainly was true, considering the average temperature had been above 90 degrees already that summer. Daily showers produced pockets of steam that rose skyward in eerie clouds from the asphalt and brick streets. Sometimes, when it started raining, the sun would still be shining. Every time that happened, Maggie thought of her favorite saying, "The devil is beating his wife if the sun is shining and the rain is raining all at the same time." Actually, it wasn't her saying at all but that of Moses Smith, her gardener and all-around helper. She had known Moses all of her life, had worked side by side with him in her father's garden as a child, and continued to do so in her own garden.

Maggie poured food and water into bowls for Brutus and Tango and ran down the stairs, checking the impulse to slide down the banister. She hit the remote for the garage door and it rolled backward slowly. Settling into her car, she turned the key. The engine started immediately, her pat to the dashboard an automatic reaction. Cautiously, she eased the car out into the silent street, making her way from the downtown warehouse district up toward Metairie Road. New Orleans would always be her home. Even Katrina could not make her leave the city. Besides, her old warehouse had remained high and dry during those awful times. New Orleans' architecture alone was worth maneuvering through the traffic jams and crowds of tourists. With little tax base other than that provided by visitors' dollars, New Orleanians accepted strangers but had less tolerance for the local criminal element that had anchored itself in some neighborhoods. A population that was mostly poor brought with it frustration, resignation, and a good deal of crime, especially when the drug dealers began their seasonal turf wars over territory. The gunslingers kept her in her lab at the coroner's office way into the night on a regular basis.

Her headlights picked up a cluster of vehicles, and Maggie parked at the end of the shortest row. A few people had wandered from their homes and lined the street, some with coffee in their cups. As she walked past them, the coffee's aroma provided a domestic quality to a surreal landscape, people appearing from and disappearing into the fog with their coffee cups. Walking up to the edge of the canal, she surveyed the officers on duty. The fog partially obscured the investigators and the victim as Maggie tried to get a better view of the woman floating in the water near the edge of the concrete-walled canal.

The victim's body could have come from anywhere. Last night's storm only complicated things. New Orleans' drainage canals were like roads connecting here and there in intricate grids, many of them shoveled out over 150 years ago by naive Irishmen who died to keep the city dry. They had come to America for the $1.50-a-day wages during one of Ireland's potato famines. Having no resistance to the local diseases, such as cholera and yellow fever, as many as 10,000 had died, some ending up in the walls of the canals. Old folks say the canals are haunted by their spirits, that late at night you can hear the Irishmen moan as the water laps against the edges of the ditches. Most likely, the sounds are just the rumblings of the giant pumps trying to move the filthy water out of the Big Easy. Lately, someone had been using the smaller canals for a dumping ground for bodies, and the *Times Picayune* was broadcasting the term "possible serial killer" in its columns.

Maggie edged closer to the canal. She slid in the mud a little as she strained to observe the investigators who were processing the scene. A few of them were drifting around the body in rubber rafts, while others hunkered at the edge of the canal, their squatting figures forming a barrier between the onlookers and death. Cameras flashed and measuring tapes snapped. They might be there for a while.

Digging her heels into the muddy ground just beyond the concrete, Maggie settled in to wait her turn to view death up close. She looked around for the coroner. Dan waved at her from a group of detectives and headed toward her. As usual, even that early in the morning his six-foot-two-inch frame was all starch and creases. Maggie felt a distant warmth begin to rise within her. She dismissed it with annoyance as he approached and bowed her back only slightly. Dan smiled his crooked little-boy smile as she resisted the urge to smile back. "Hey, Maggie, thanks for coming. The boys down there will be finished in a few minutes."

"What's the story here, Dan?"

"She was spotted less than an hour ago by a bread man on his first delivery of the day. He's over there, still sick. His stop to relieve himself in the canal probably cost him his shift, but at least he called the police. I don't want to bias you, Maggie, but she looks a lot like the others. Young, possibly a prostitute, but we have no way of knowing yet. We don't even know who she is.

Maybe the autopsy will help." Someone called to Dan and he turned to leave, an attempt to touch Maggie's shoulder aborted in mid-flight, either by the way she looked at him or his own second thoughts.

Maggie went back to casing the area. Those who lingered had nothing better to do. A couple of street people with everything they owned in purloined grocery carts, several older residents who may have spent their entire lives there, and others with closed faces whose reasons for gawking at death perhaps unknown even to themselves. She had walked through that area many times in the past. Just like the Irish Channel, the neighborhood where she grew up in the 1970s, it hadn't changed for the better. Back then, she was Margaret Rose Muller, with a French and Irish Catholic mother and a beer-swilling German-Indian father. At 17 she'd changed her last name to her mother's maiden name, Andrepont, when her mother died and she left home. Her old neighborhood dated back to the nineteenth century when the Irish packed two to four families into one hastily constructed shotgun house.

Two weeks ago, Rodney Durham, a local film producer, had come around wanting Maggie to be part of his documentary on Irish Catholic success stories from the neighborhood. He seemed especially interested in her work with the coroner's office. Her reluctance to cooperate had only piqued his interest even more. Though evading him was getting harder and harder, he indicated he would make the film with or without her cooperation. Currently, it was without. She couldn't figure out his angle. Was it her recent involvement with a couple of gangster-related deaths, the one or two voodoo whodunnits, or the rap artist's dismemberment that caught his interest?

She had left the old neighborhood behind her years

earlier when waiting tables, delivering pizza, and a series of other odd jobs helped put her through four years of school in anthropology at Tulane. She had just started to panic over her federal loans when a scholarship call came from Arizona State. Out of seven master's applications, ASU came through. She jumped at the graduate assistantship they offered.

Back in New Orleans for more than 15 years, she had built a fairly successful urban archaeology consulting business, Subsurface Investigations. Every time a new construction project started, someone hit the foundation of an old building, a nineteenth-century toilet, or a lost cemetery. With the help of her archaeology partner, Lucas Evans, and volunteers, Maggie had dug holes all over the city, recovering bits and pieces of New Orleans' past. Dishes, guns, Confederate money, human bones, and more. Lately, though, she'd been spending most of her time on forensic work. At ASU she had trained in bioarchaeology and forensic anthropology, digging up the ancient dead and profiling the recently dead. But the dry climate in Arizona had not prepared her for decaying bodies in South Louisiana, where it was hot, wet, suffocating for almost 300 days of the year. One thing was certain, if it was dead in New Orleans, it was going fast, human or otherwise.

But most of the time her job was straightforward, figuring out age, sex, and race of an unidentified set of bones. Trauma was a little different. If somebody grabbed somebody else and put a gun, a knife, or a club to him or her, distinguishing one type of wound from another and which came first could get more complicated. Crimes of passion, the books called them. Maggie called them crimes of meanness. Sometimes, that was the only explanation that made sense.

Recently she had been hoping to wind up her local

work because she was anticipating the start of a new bioarchaeology project on the other side of the world, but someone kept dumping women's bodies in New Orleans' canals. Maggie figured the woman's body was probably ripe with the gases that formed from the bacteria working overtime in her trash-filled, watery grave.

Awareness of someone in her personal space brought Maggie back to the present and to full attention.

"Hey, Maggie, look at your toes, and you'll end up with a bloody nose," a raspy, familiar voice whispered in her ear.

With a strong urge to glance at her feet, and only slightly irritated, Maggie swung around and looked up into Jimmy O'Malley's tanned, angular face, a Camel dangling from the corner of his mouth and his big brown cow eyes dancing. "For God's sake, Jimmy, cut the dumb rhymes this early in the morning."

"Sorry, Maggie," he said, sounding a little hurt. "What's going on? Who called *you* out? She doesn't look like she's been dead long enough to end up in your lab."

"Get back behind that row of yellow tape over there before you get in trouble. Dan called me, and, besides, you know I can't tell a *Picayune* reporter anything about a case no matter how long we've known each other. What is it now? Through three wives? No, wait a minute, it's almost July. Surely it must be four." Even as Maggie said the words, she regretted them. She was jumpy, especially with last night's Santeria bathtub act and the puzzle of the canal women. She was in a foul mood way too early in the day and had taken it out on one of the few people in the world she could call her friend. She felt a twinge of self-loathing.

"Ouch! I'll take my limericks any day over your anteater tongue," Jimmy fired back.

"I'm sorry, you big goon, but you startled me."

"Boy, if that's how you react these days when you're just startled, I don't want to see you really riled up."

"Very funny," she said, but he had touched a nerve. She was edgy, no doubt in part because of the three other bodies in the last couple of weeks that were similar to this one. She was angry at such a waste of human life. The watery grave added even more problems, often obscuring details vital to identification and determining cause of death.

Maggie was just about to tell Jimmy she owed him lunch for the sharp retort, a habit they'd had since their teenage years when they promised to always be friends and never be mad at each other more than 24 hours in a row. But they were interrupted by a young, neatly dressed city policeman firmly nudging Jimmy with his clipboard, pointing him to a spot behind the yellow tape. Jimmy headed toward the tape, giving Maggie a forgiving smile and a "See ya" salute just as the men at the edge of the canal began to move.

Sidney Snyder, the lead coroner's investigator, picked up the head end of the black body bag. Joey, his dim-eyed assistant, carried the feet. Their climb up the slanted concrete walls of the canal seemed effortless.

"Sidney," Maggie said, "let me take a quick look before she goes to autopsy, would you? Dan called me out."

"Oh, Miss Maggie, you know Doc Browning don't want you or nobody else touching any body until after she's seen it."

"Yeah, I know, but I promise not to touch, just to

11

look. O.K.?"

His eyes said yes, and he rested the body bag on the gurney near Maggie. He snipped the coroner's plastic seal. Maggie unzipped the bag cautiously, as though it mattered to the one inside. Sidney held the flap as she looked into the swollen face of a young black woman, not more than 25 years old. She appeared limp, probably having gone in and out of rigor hours earlier. Maggie's eyes moved down the body. The abdomen was distended, just enough to make her float. In a few more hours in this heat she would be totally unrecognizable, but for now, most of her facial features were still intact.

Snapping four quick photos, Maggie noted the victim's closely cropped hair and a small jagged scar on her chin. She wore a red halter top and denim shorts. No shoes. Her fingernails were well manicured but unpolished. Maggie wanted to raise her arms and look, but she didn't. She had promised Sidney. The right side of the woman's head was injured, probably blunt force. Most likely, she would get her later anyway. Then she could check under the arms.

Maggie helped Sidney rezip the body bag, watching the blowflies that had begun to gather. They're quick in the Deep South, sometimes arriving just minutes after a person dies. Where did that many come from so fast? "Not this time, you little spoilers," Maggie said to herself, waving them aside as she conjured the unpleasant image of the woman's body had it been found on dry land accompanied by the flies' offspring. She made a mental note to tell the forensic entomologists, the bug people, that she had seen the flies hovering, just in case some eggs hatched into maggots in the next eight to twelve hours and skewed their estimate of time since death.

Maggie's cell phone vibrated, giving her a start.

She disliked cell phones, always being connected to the world, but Dan had talked her into it. He agreed to pay the monthly fee if he could just find her when he needed her. Anthropologist on a rope. She recognized the caller as Maura Stone. She ignored the call. What in the world? What could she possibly want at this hour? How did Maura get her cell number anyway? She wasn't safe even this early from Maura's uncanny ability to locate her. Volunteer extraordinaire. Constantly calling, always wanting to help, relentlessly urging Maggie to let her assist in the lab on the archaeology projects, her unusual accent one or two syllables away from being familiar. Maura had appeared as Medusa in Maggie's dreams one night. Ever since, Maggie couldn't look at Maura's straight black hair without seeing ringlets of snakes, their heads snapping back and forth as she made her way across a room.

In reality, at forty plus Maura could still turn many a head, her smile marred only by a peculiar inverted "v" notched into the biting edge of her upper right canine. But it was her eyes Maggie noticed most. They were dark pools. Maggie figured men could almost drown in their depths.

She thought of the old saying, "If you dream it, it will come true." She hoped not, and not just because of Maura. Last night right before the ambulances almost punctured her eardrums, all of her front teeth seemed to be falling out. That dream probably was a result of one of two things: either her recent forensic case where someone had tried to pry the gold crowns off a murdered drug dealer's upper central incisors or the abundance of Tabasco sauce she had added to the crawfish étouffée one of the morgue assistants had brought to her office. In any case, she was trying to avoid Maura. She didn't want her to learn about the new archaeology project. No amateurs allowed.

Maggie watched the investigators load the body bag into the white van, its back doors closing loudly. They eased the unmarked vehicle off the curb and drove away. In less than two minutes, they'd be surrounded by the few people eager to be first on the job for the day and others who were just going home, all of them unaware that the van in front of them carried a murder victim.

She glanced around for Jimmy but he was gone, slipping away to meet a deadline she figured. Though he was James O'Malley, ace reporter for the *Times Pica-yune*, he hadn't changed much since elementary school when he would tap her on the shoulder, whisper his newest rhyme in her ear, then dart across the school-yard.

The rest of the crowd began to retreat from the yellow tape, gathering in smaller groups down the street. They appeared to be waiting for something else to happen. It wasn't happening there, not that day.

Maggie lingered at the edge of the canal, just looking. The fog had begun to burn off. A breeze caused the water to ripple slightly, reminding her of where she might be in a few days. If her proposal was accepted, she would have the project of her dreams. It hinged on two things. One was keeping her old friend, Lucas Evans, her long-time assistant and one of the best bioarchaeologists in the country, away from alcohol long enough to pass the required physical examination. The other was approval of her credentials by the antiquities commission in Rome. Approval of her role in the project might be fairly simple. It all boiled down to a recent phone call to her office.

"Hello, Margaret Rose," he said that day when she answered her phone. Her stomach had gone soft. Eduardo Philippe Martusa. He was the only one who called her by her full name. Fifteen years fell away.

"Eduardo! Where are you? Are you here in the States?" She couldn't keep the excitement out of her voice.

"No, Maggie, I'm in Rome. I just wanted to make sure you were in town. Do me a favor. Stay home a little late tomorrow. I want to talk with you about something exciting. How would you like to come here to Italy to do a project for me?"

"How can I do that? Aren't local bioarchaeologists the only ones who can direct projects there?"

"No, those policies changed years ago. Besides, this is special. I need you soon. Are you interested?"

"Of course."

"Fine, I'll call you tomorrow around noon your time with more details. And, Maggie, you sound great. Talk to you soon."

Maggie had leaned back in her chair. Arizona. Graduate school. Eduardo. His dark eyes, his hesitant smile, his strong hands. Eduardo, whose English was broken at best back then, and who still talked her into helping him with his class, Old World Archaeology and the Rise of Man. By midterm of the semester, Maggie had learned a thing or two about the rise of man. Sex with Eduardo was the closest she had ever come to really making love. Though he was not the first or the last, he remained the most memorable. She had no idea at the time that he was from one of Italy's oldest and wealthiest families and had come to graduate school in the States to gain an American perspective on preservation of historic structures. But she doubted even Eduardo could have predicted that at such an early age he would become Minister of Antiquities for all of Italy. They had sort of stayed in touch. Every year on the anniversary of their graduation from ASU, Eduardo sent roses. "For An Untamed Irish Rose" was all the card ever said.

The crowd near the canal scene began to break up, a few closed faces glancing Maggie's way. She looked toward the canal once more, then turned and walked to her Karmann Ghia. Its appearance and size often had saved her when sheriff's deputies suggested she transport human remains to her lab. She told them, "They just won't fit." Besides, she had smelled officers' cars when they'd been forced to transport the not so recently dead. The odor of death could linger indefinitely, especially if it made its way into the upholstery. Once there, you could never escape its faint reminder of where everyone would end up. She smelled enough of that in her lab. When asked to describe the odor of death, she acknowledged that, to her, it smelled like multiple things. Uncooked chicken parts you forgot were in your garbage until the next day. Inedible, aged cheese. Stagnant water from flowers left too long in a vase. Rotting potatoes. All rolled into one. It was, admittedly, a hard odor to capture with words, but once you had smelled it, you recognized it instantly if you ever encountered it again. And Maggie had, hundreds of times.

Maggie's car was special to her and she did not want the smell of death to be present in that car. She had purchased the Karmann Ghia from Carl's Classic Cars in Belle Chasse, across the river from New Orleans. Carl's was better known as CC's but had been dubbed "BB's" for "Bubba's Behemoths" by Dan. The car's guts were Volkswagen, its body design Italian. Exotic to Maggie. Bondo on the holes in the fenders had helped its appearance, but it was polka-dotted with the orange paint and the beige Bondo. When it rained, the Bondo seemed to glow, especially at night. Restoration had stopped there. Moses, her old friend and gardener, shied away from it. He didn't think it was reliable. Of course, long road trips were out. But it worked just fine in crowded streets and could slip into the smallest of parking spaces. With the top down, Maggie could drive through the Quarter, listening to the sounds she had grown up with. Lately, they'd been laced with the obscenities the new generation of boozers had brought to the city with them, thinking their language made them sound tough and streetwise. A good bar of lye soap for their bodies and their mouths. That's what Mama would have said, Maggie thought.

Maggie started her car. She drove from the scene and headed toward the Garden District. On St. Charles Avenue, fewer people than usual were stirring that morning. Probably a little too much partying the night before. New Orleans has several hundred thousand people packed together in rectangular-shaped grids running from the river, spreading out in all directions. The Mississippi River cut a semicircle into the delta thousands of years ago, creating a crescent-shaped bowl into which nineteenth-century ships dumped immigrants by the thousands. The surrounding swampy land invited every species of bug imaginable to take up residence and nibble on the unsuspecting inhabitants.

Epidemics were a part of life in the early years, and the rich as well as the poor often died if they remained in the city during the summer months. Those who could headed out of town until the weather cooled, trying to avoid diseases and the incessant smell of garbage.

Passing Melpomene, Terpsichore, St. Andrew, and Josephine Streets in the Lower Garden District, Maggie slowed to a crawl as she turned up First. Driving in the District in the early mornings often calmed her. Thinking about the lives of those behind the shuttered windows and garden walls reminded her of her mother. The Garden District was two miles upriver or "uptown" from the Vieux Carré, the main destination for most tourists visiting New Orleans. Just enough distance between the two to filter out the drunks and the trash they left behind, at least part of the time.

When Maggie was young, her mother would take her to the Garden District on Sunday afternoons. They'd walk up and down the blocks of Felicity, Louisiana, First, and Second Streets, memorizing the old homes, whispering about their wrought-iron gates and half-veiled gardens late into the evening.

Though she made a decent living, Maggie's yearly income had not put her in a position to buy a big home in the Garden District. Since she needed a lot of space, she took advantage of the trend to refurbish the buildings in the Warehouse District, close to the river. Following almost fifty years on the heels of those in New York, developers in New Orleans had begun to restore the old warehouses. Maggie had bought in early, having one of the older buildings to herself and a thirty-year mortgage that went with it.

Her first floor was for storage and her Karmann Ghia. Two large rooms and a bath, all with heart pine floors and great windows, filled her second-floor living area. The summer heat could be a problem, but fans hanging from foot-thick cypress beams helped at night. Some nights she would even turn off her air conditioner and open the oversized windows. They let in an occasional breeze, punctuated by the inevitable odor of automobile fumes and garbage. Though mosquitoes the size of horseflies buzzed against the window screens, anyone else wanting to enter uninvited had to scale the flat walls and be introduced to Brutus, 165 pounds of putty until someone went near Maggie. She had raised the Great Dane from a pup and spent several sleepless nights with a hot-water bottle keeping him company when she first took him from his mother. His sidekick, Tango, came from the back alley. Tango was no ordinary cat. According to the vet, he was a short-haired tabby and at least five years old when Maggie found him. Often, Tango charged with wild abandon across the old pine floors, his sideways maneuvers reminiscent of the dance for which he was named. His ragged ears suggested he was also streetwise. Neutered, he was a little nicer now, but he tolerated very few.

Together, Brutus and Tango patrolled Maggie's courtyard. She had purchased the small lot adjacent to her building when it was left vacant after the termite-ridden building that stood there was demolished. Though her budget was stretched to its limit, her courtyard was a little slice of heaven. Over the years, Moses had helped her fill the courtyard with plants they had rescued from the trash dumpster by Trosclair's nursery. Though raising a grandchild alone after the death of his wife and daughter, Moses still found time to help Maggie. He was fulfilling a promise he had made to Maggie's mother years before. He kept her anchored and had, in fact, positioned himself as her personal therapist.

It all started with, "Miss Maggie, if you'd just take these clippers and cut here, here, and here, this wisteria and jasmine would grow right up this wall, and you'd feel a lot better, too."

The next time, he said, "Miss Maggie, you wanna help me with this bag of dirt?"

Before she knew it, Maggie had been drawn in, occasionally watching *Your Green Thumb* on the Learning Channel late at night when she couldn't sleep. The only thing Moses asked of her was that she not water the plants twice a day. Though the bananas and indigo seemed to love it, the roses had a distressed look. They had reached an agreement. He watered. She snipped dead leaves. Of course, she watered, too, and he would just shake his head and smile.

"Miss Maggie, you just hardheaded," he would say, chuckling to himself, obviously pleased that she had taken even the slightest interest in something other than "those poor lost souls."

Maggie drove slowly through the Garden District, her attention returning to the new Jane Doe from the canal and then wandering to another set of canals, those in a place she had only visited briefly five years ago, Venice. When she was younger, if someone had suggested that she might travel to the city of canals and lovers at all, she would have scoffed at the idea. But she did go there, reluctantly. Venice was part of a whirlwind package tour of Europe with which she had rewarded herself when her business hit its ten-year anniversary. Once she arrived in Venice, she hadn't wanted to leave. The architecture, the canals, the people. That trip had also been in July. The fishy odors and dank waters of the endless canals were familiar smells. She felt at home. Now she hoped to return.

A drawing of Venice that she had bought at a junk shop on Decatur Street hung on the wall above her kitchen sink and captured San Marcos Square in the heart of Venice as seen from the lagoon. In the piazza was a campanile, just across from the Doge's Palace. The tower had begun to lean, its base undermined by age and by oil drilling in the lagoon, Eduardo had told her in his first phone call. A support of some kind had to be erected to prevent the tower from falling. Though most of the tower had been rebuilt about a hundred years earlier, the ground floor of the old campanile, first constructed a thousand or so years before, had remained intact. When workmen tried to shore up the sinking base, they discovered a hidden chamber below street level. It was sandwiched in among the gigantic wooden pilings that had been driven deep into the ground to stabilize the original structure. "Inside the small tower chamber," Eduardo said, "are skeletons everywhere, Maggie, maybe ten or more, some like mummies."

The work on the tower had stopped, but it had to be completed. Antonio Lista, the bioarchaeologist who had begun an evaluation of the skeletal remains, suffered a heart attack in the hot and cramped working conditions. He had just found out from his doctors that returning to the project could be suicide. He would not be back. Italy's other bioarchaeologists with experience in such recoveries were at Herculaneum, where as many as fifty skeletons had been discovered huddled against a wall. The small amphitheater in which they were found was encapsulated by lava when Mount Vesuvius erupted in AD 79, covering Herculaneum and her more famous sister city nearby, Pompeii. The research team could not leave to assist Eduardo.

"The bones from the tower must be removed and analyzed quickly, Maggie. Their final disposition is not settled. They'll probably be buried in one of Venice's church cemeteries in about a month. I need your help."

Maggie recalled the first time he'd asked for her help, aggravated with herself for blushing all these years later, glad he was unable to see her face and her fingers that trembled slightly as she pressed them against her bottom lip.

The odds of such a project being handed over to

her had to be phenomenal. She had called Lucas Evans immediately, hoping he was in a drying-out phase and ready to work his site mapping magic.

"Lucas, how would you like to be surrounded by still waters in paradise?"

"Well, Maggie, I'm not dead yet, but that sounds like heaven. What did you have in mind?"

For just a moment, a hint of his old humor had returned.

"It's Venice in July, and you always loved fish. How about it?"

"Oh, Maggie, I don't know if I'm ready for this."

"Of course you're ready." She sounded pushy, she knew, but she was hoping to accomplish two things: securing the best partner she had ever had for a major project and getting his mind off Amy.

Until a year ago, Maggie never went into the field without Lucas to help with the maps. His site maps, with their blend of simplicity and attention to essential detail, had made their way into archaeology textbooks. She had relied on his help in cemetery projects as well as in forensic burials. He was the best, but he hadn't worked on a major project since last year when Amy died. She had been hit one evening in the Quarter when a drunken driver ran up on a curb, injuring Lucas and leaving Amy to die in his arms. They'd been married ten years, and Amy was the love of his life. She was also his mapping partner. Since it happened, he'd been drinking too much and spending the insurance money on prostitutes in the Quarter. Recently, he'd also become enamored with tattoos, and now two ugly gargoyles glared from his chest, his nipples incorporated into their exaggerated grins.

Maggie had run into Lucas one night at Mother's

Restaurant, where she had gone for some of the best catfish in the city. The young woman on his arm was as drunk as he was and not the slightest bit embarrassed when he threw open his shirt to show Maggie his "body art." She found herself annoyed by the gargoyles' grotesque appearance yet drawn by a strange attraction. She would make him keep his shirt on in Venice, but for now she was just keeping her fingers and toes crossed that he would be able to pass the physical.

Fingers and toes, the latest body from the canal. If the woman was a prostitute as the investigators speculated, she certainly didn't fit the typical profile. Something wasn't right. She had no tracks on her arms. She wasn't unusually thin. According to Dan, no one on the street had been reported missing.

What about the other three victims? Two of them were local women, one a known prostitute, the other an accountant at a college. The third was still a Jane Doe. Two of the three also shared something distinctive in their physical profile: small, peculiar tattoos.

The prostitute's body, the first one found in the canals, was badly decomposed. The twenty-pound cinder block tied to her left leg had kept her down only long enough to distort her features. The forensic dentist identified her with dental x-rays, one silver amalgam filling in the biting surface of her lower left wisdom tooth, the only link to who she was. Many of her other teeth had needed repair work. If she'd once had tattoos, no one could tell. Much of her skin had melted away in the summer heat. The turtles had taken care of the rest.

Maggie and Doc Browning had almost overlooked the tattoo on the third victim, the bookkeeper, though her fair skin was a pale canvas for the small circle with a jagged line in its center etched into the tender area between the fourth and fifth toes of her right foot.

The tattoo on the second victim, who still remained unidentified, had gone unnoticed by everyone, including Maggie, hidden near the natural hair under her arms. The second victim and the bookkeeper had been found within twenty-four hours of one another. Maggie had gone over to a local funeral home to check out that Jane Doe. Just a hunch after seeing the other tattoo.

The mortician had donated a funeral for the Jane Doe, though she would not be buried until all efforts to identify her had been exhausted. He had cleaned her body before he embalmed her. The small tattoo in her left armpit resembled a dark blue mole. A closer look with a magnifying glass provided a better view. It was also a circle, but it had a wavy line across the center. Geez, that must have hurt, under the arm like that, Maggie thought, recalling the prick of the needle and the sting it carried with it.

Chapter 2

The morning paper bounced over her courtyard wall as Maggie raised her first cup of Community Coffee to her lips. Strong and black. Brutus looked up for just a moment and then returned to his breakfast, inhaling the dry food with his usual noisy crunches. Tango never moved from his window perch. Maggie usually took the paper with her to the lab and read it there, but she was curious about the new canal case. Easing down the stairs with her coffee, she tried not to spill it on her scrubs. She didn't always wear scrubs to work but had a feeling she'd get the girl's case today right after autopsy. Dan, in his official coroner's voice, had asked her to leave all tissue on the first three victims, what there was left of it, but she figured he was getting anxious now. He rarely made direct requests of her, always allowing her to just do her job and then provide him with the results of her anthropological analysis on each case. For years, he seemed uncomfortable with having to exert authority over her and usually wound up apologizing for a direct request. Few knew how kind he could be. Maggie decided she might as well go prepared to macerate the body and shower and change at the morgue after work. That way, she would be ready to work on the case if he requested it.

Maggie's forensic anthropology lab was one large room in the parish morgue, and Dan let her use the space for other projects as well. She and Lucas were the only ones with keys. Though the space was cramped, they had the advantage of assistance from the chemists and other trace evidence experts who worked down the hall. The chemists' only complaint was an occasional assault on their olfactories when Maggie had to clean an especially ripe body. She and Lucas often worked late into the night to keep the odors down in the old building, sometimes just getting started on a case when everyone else was leaving for the day. Then, as quickly as possible, they would freeze the putrefactive soft tissue for future burial with the rest of the body if the person was identified quickly. If a case stayed a John or Jane Doe for more than a few months, they cremated the soft tissue in the incinerator across town.

Last year's refurbishment of the morgue had resulted in a new fume hood for Maggie's lab, which helped considerably with the odors, but she felt her days at the morgue were numbered, especially if Dan left office any time soon.

The headlines of the *Times-Picayune* jumped out at her: "Up Pops Another, Just Like the Other." Jimmy's perverse limericks again. His byline as the paper's main crime reporter confirmed he had penned the article. How did he get away with such language? The *Times-Pic* had always seemed fairly conservative about such things. Maybe the deaths had them rattled, too, and they were a little antsy for something to report.

Maggie started reading: "The coroner, the chief of

police, and the sheriff are setting up a special task force to determine whether the bodies found in New Orleans' drainage canals are related cases. The cause of death for the latest victim awaits results of today's autopsy. Forensic anthropologist Maggie Andrepont will participate in the investigation."

That Jimmy, always giving her a plug. So Dan hadn't been able to get Dr. Patsy Browning to do an autopsy yesterday. Otherwise, he would have called her in. She hoped the wait wasn't going to compromise valuable evidence. Pathologists. A few autopsies under their belt and they all became prima donnas.

She finished her coffee, rubbed Brutus and Tango's heads and loaded her Karmann Ghia. If she was lucky, Browning might let her observe the autopsy. The pathologist still acted a little peeved when Dan called Maggie in on a case, but Maggie always discussed her findings with her. Putrefactive soft tissue could hide so many things. After removing all of it and reconstructing damaged bones, Maggie's main job in many cases, a slightly different picture might emerge in terms of bullet trajectory or number of wounds. Lately, Browning had been coming around.

Pulling onto Tulane Avenue, Maggie felt her cell phone vibrate. She looked at the caller. Maura. She let it keep going, then stop. Might as well call her back. Maura wouldn't give up until she did. She jerked up her cell phone and punched in Maura's number. Maura picked up after just two rings. "Hello." Her husky greeting, obviously practiced, was lost on Maggie.

"Maura. Maggie. What's up?" Maggie said sharply. She hated to talk on the phone and drive at the same time.

"Oh, Maggie, thanks for calling me back." Maura's words came quick, breathless. "Did you get that woman from the canal? I just wanted to let you know I could help you if you like."

"Hold it, Maura. I don't know yet if I'll *get* the girl. If I do, I have my partner, Lucas, and more help from mortuary students over at Delgado. I didn't know you were interested in forensic cases. You said you just wanted to help on historical projects. By the way, how did you get my cell number?" Loud noises came from the other end of the line.

"What's that, Maggie? I'll have to call you back later."

Pulling back into the center lane, Maggie barely missed a truck loaded with bottled water. She could see Jimmy's lead tomorrow: "Forensic Anthropologist's Head Just above Water on Dry Land."

Maura Stone. Why the sudden interest in forensics? Most people just wanted to hear the stories, not touch the decaying bodies. Where had she come from anyway? Maggie's first meeting with Maura had been about a year before. It was at the open house celebrating Dan's remodeling job at the morgue. Dan had introduced them. She would have to find the business card Maura had left with her. She seemed to recall that it simply said "Consultant." Dan could tell her more about Maura. But Maura was just one among many who thought they wanted to be involved with analyzing the dead. That interest usually waned when they saw death up close. Many students never returned after only one session in her lab. If the smell didn't get them, the cheese skippers—the jumping maggots—usually did.

Chapter 3

Maggie parked in her regular spot at the coroner's office. Straddling the concrete between the parking lot and the sidewalk, she left just enough room for someone to edge past without being forced into the street. Her Karmann Ghia's notoriety helped stem the flow of tickets associated with her obvious offense.

Glancing toward the sky, she decided to raise her new ragtop before going to the lab. Its shiny surface had not yet been dulled by pollution and constant downpours. It stood out in stark contrast to the car's imperfect fenders and hood.

As Maggie headed toward the lab, Sidney Snyder walked out the door, the flash of his lighter an instant confirmation of his lapse into an old habit. Sometimes, Maggie wondered why Dan chose him as lead coroner's investigator. Of course, it was none of her business who Dan chose for any position. Sidney just irritated her with some of his actions. "Hey, Miss Maggie," he said, his eyes wandering to places other than her face, lingering longer than appropriate. "You best hurry if you're gonna make the first cut."

Maggie raised her hand in a brief hello-goodbye salute, then hurried past him and down the corridor to Room A. She almost stopped to ask him if his headaches had returned but saved it for another time, aggravated by his roving eyes. She knocked on the door and waited for a reply before entering the autopsy room.

A detective opened the door, his crisp white shirt and new suit an immediate giveaway. Dr. Patsy Browning, the coroner's only board certified forensic pathologist, glanced up, motioning for Maggie to come in. The lab tech was unzipping the body bag. "Maggie, good to see you," Browning said, her voice somewhat muffled behind her mask. "Dan called and said you might be here. Let's get on with this."

The detectives parted like a wave, allowing Maggie to get closer to the autopsy table. The technician finished unzipping the bag, carefully positioning the top flap to prevent fluids from escaping at the corners and spilling onto the floor.

The body's odor seared into Maggie's brain. She quickly grabbed a disposable mask and gown from a nearby table. Though Sidney normally would have transferred the body directly to the morgue's cooler yesterday, it must have sat out for a while. Maybe he thought the autopsy was imminent. Perhaps that explained the pained look on his face. Browning must have chewed his rear.

The body had changed significantly. The midsection had swollen even more. The tongue was thick and filled the oral cavity. The eyes bulged from their sockets. Death saturated the room.

One young officer, probably about to witness his

first autopsy of a putrefactive body, stepped back into a corner, his face reflecting anxiety and a lack of confidence that he could make it through the next two hours. Others in the room shifted uncomfortably, their soles scraping in unison on the concrete floor. It was going to be a long and unpleasant morning.

Browning announced, "I'm about to begin recording. Unless you want to be a part of my final report, please keep your breakfast down and your mouth shut."

She began a routine Maggie had come to know well. Leaning toward the mike, she spoke, "Young, black female, under the age of thirty. Small, 100–110 pounds." Stretching a measuring tape from the crown of the victim's head to her heel, she added, "Approximately five feet three inches tall. Short cropped hair, one-inch scar on chin. Wearing a red halter top and blue denim shorts. Shorts and top appear to be in place, no signs of disturbance."

Browning then observed, "An apparent blunt force trauma to right temporal region, just posterior to eye orbit and above zygomatic arch."

Picking up the scissors, she cut the halter top away, snapping each strap at the shoulder and then cutting through the left side seam. Maggie watched intently as Browning moved toward the shorts. They had a looped waistband, front zipper, and a metal button at the top. Browning couldn't undo the button because of the swollen abdomen. Instead, she cut through the denim fabric, beginning near the lower outside seam of the left leg and working her way upward toward the waist. She did the same on the right. Folding the front of the pants toward the knees, she nodded for Maggie to help her as she slipped them from beneath the body like a soiled diaper. Cotton panties remained. They stretched tight across the pubic region, rolling slightly due to the swelling. Two quick snips with the scissors, and she removed them in the same fashion as the shorts. Maggie helped her with the halter top and together they rolled the body slightly toward its left side. Browning gave the top a quick tug. It slipped easily into her hands.

"Maggie, grab that evidence bag by you, please," Browning said. Browning folded the clothes carefully and placed them in the paper evidence bag as Maggie held it open. Browning then sealed it and scribbled notations on the side with one fluid movement. Maggie knew the rape kit would come next. Browning always followed the same routine.

Browning sampled the vaginal, cervical, and anal areas with swabs, sealing the swabs in the containers provided by the tech standing nearby. Placing them in another evidence bag, she added one more set of her initials with something close to a flourish. She passed them along for storage.

The room was quiet, the breathing expectant. The detectives moved in and out of view of the body. A couple of them turned their heads away from the table when Browning took a small comb and moved it back and forth several times through the victim's pubic hair. She placed the loose hairs in an envelope. They might include the murderer's hairs if he'd pressed his body there.

Browning lifted the victim's left hand and then the right, looking for broken nails, abrasions, someone else's skin under the nails. Maggie knew that a few foreign skin cells could provide enough DNA to catch a killer. The freshly manicured nails gave Browning pause and she glanced Maggie's way. Maggie nodded slightly, acknowledging that she had also noticed the professional manicure. Hands say a lot about a person, Maggie thought. The victim's hands once were smooth but now were wrinkled from the canal water. Well cared for, they were way too young to be on an autopsy table. Browning began clipping the nails, each one making a soft clicking sound as it landed in the bottom of the paper evidence bag the autopsy technician held in place.

Finishing her preliminary assessment, Browning nodded at Maggie and they both shifted their positions, Maggie on the victim's right side, Browning on the left. They inched toward the victim's head. For just a moment, Maggie wanted to turn away from the case. Most of her cases were much more advanced in their decomposition than this one. She rarely got to see their eyes, but this one had eyes.

Browning checked the eyes for petechiae, small hemorrhages that could indicate constriction of the veins of the neck. Often, they were associated with strangulation. She lingered at the eyes for a moment. While carefully drawing fluid with a hypodermic, she recorded, "Probably too late for humor help." The eye fluid, or vitreous humor, could be used in various diagnostic tests, one of which pinpointed time since death by measuring the potassium level. Nature was not on their side.

The throat showed no obvious abrasions or bruises, but Browning gently palpated the region directly below the chin. "Hyoid in place, no signs of bruising or breakage. Will remove later for closer analysis." Again, a glance in Maggie's direction. Browning knew Maggie always checked out the hyoid bone in such cases. The small horseshoe-shaped bone helped to anchor the tongue in place and strangulation could damage it. Though it started out as three bones and generally fused into one by the age of 35 or so, it might never fuse. That lack of fusion could be mistaken as a break, but confirmation came with removal of the tissue.

The time had come for Maggie to give Browning a wide berth and she was glad to do it. Once the body was open and the internal viscera exposed, as the pathologist, only Browning had the expertise to sort through the decomposing organs and figure out if they could provide information about cause of death.

Starting near the lateral end of the right inferior collar bone, Browning's incision moved toward the midline and across the body to the edge of the left armpit. Turning downward, her scalpel traveled the left side of the thorax to the region just below the navel. She then cut across the body to the right side. Unlike the traditional Y incision she usually made, this flap procedure opened the chest like a door. It was her preferred technique for waterlogged bodies that would gape open in the middle when she attempted to stitch together putrefactive tissue in the traditional manner after autopsy.

Using her right forefinger as a guide, Browning sliced through the outer layers of skin and fascia like a surgeon. The scalpel's new blade caught the light from above and flashed briefly. She cautiously peeled back the tissue covering the chest cavity, cutting through the thin layer of golden fat. Gesturing for Maggie to follow her, she walked to the wall-mounted view box to examine the chest x-rays made earlier by the technician. "Maggie, do you see any old fractures that have healed or any new ones? I don't want to use the bone pliers on the ribs if there is something going on there."

To herself, Maggie said, "Oh, I like you and what you are doing." To Browning, she simply shook her head. Browning was young, but good. Sometimes Maggie had seen more experienced pathologists just use the pliers or a Stryker saw to break through the chest midway into the ribs, snapping the sternal ends of the ribs as they went. Their haste to get through as many cases as possible in one day could compromise any obscured trauma in the rib area and result in loss of evidence, especially if the tissue was putrefactive. What was even more unusual was that Browning was placing Maggie on equal footing, including her in part of the actual autopsy procedure. Maggie felt giddy, her earlier discomfort with the autopsy of one so young temporarily pushed to the back of her mind.

Browning returned to the table and cut through the rib sections adjacent to the sternum, placing the sternum and rib ends attached to it on a tray. The mass rested flat, the youthful cartilage and bone resembling a spiderlike creature with irregular appendages. The internal organs lay exposed. She then drew blood from the left subclavian artery just below the collar bone and filled three small tubes she had already labeled. She was ready for the organs.

One by one, Browning carefully removed the heart, the liver, the gallbladder, the lungs, the spleen. Weighing, sectioning, and sampling each, she temporarily placed them in the tub at the foot of the table. Later, they would be returned to the body cavity. The skin-flap door would then be stretched back across the chest and sewn securely with thick twine. With burial clothing in place, a family would never have to witness the disfiguring cuts.

Continuing her search for clues, Browning opened and examined the stomach, "Ate last meal shortly before death, undigested food in stomach," she recorded. "Maggie, tell me what you think this is," she said, pointing to the contents of the stomach.

Maggie edged closer and looked. She made an educated guess. "Tofu?"

"Exactly what I thought," Browning said, taking a sample of the material.

"Young, clean as a whistle, health food, fresh manicure—what the hell?" Maggie thought. She was dying to raise the arms, but, again, she stepped back. They were on the pathologist's turf. Though Browning was including her in the procedure, she was not about to initiate any act that could possibly offend her. Forensic anthropologists rarely had the opportunity that Browning was giving her.

Browning didn't notice Maggie's impatience as she examined the left and right kidneys. She then made a vertical incision through the skin from just below the navel to the terminal pubic region. Once more, she quickly sliced through near-surface fascia. Probing the various folds of the colon with her scalpel handle, she was careful not to rupture the gut, the area into which pathologists rarely ventured. Finally, she finished exposing the entire pubic region with the blade. She drew liquid from the bladder with a syringe and handed the sample to her tech. He released a little of the urine onto a small, white cotton strip, watching the tab turn a yellow green. He then used a color guide to look for evidence of bilirubins, ketones, and other compounds excreted into the urine at various intervals after death.

Next, Browning examined the reproductive organs while speaking into the mike, "This young woman most likely just finished menstruating. Nothing remarkable here except that probably she has never given birth. The opening to the cervix is small and round, the uterus plum like."

Browning walked toward the other end of the table, grabbing a face shield as she went. She was ready for the head. A new scalpel blade easily cut through the thin scalp tissue in a coronal cut from side to side, just behind the ears. She used both hands to peel the tissue from the bone. The youthful periosteum, the or ganic sheath covering bone, offered the only resistance. Looking something like a welder with her face shield in place to protect herself from body fluids and carcinogenic bone dust, she picked up the saw and cut out the top of the skull, the calotte. The smell of singed bone penetrated Maggie's mask.

In deference to the wound on the right side of the head, Browning removed less of the skull cap than usual, notching the bone in the frontal area just above the center of the forehead for ease of replacement. She then slipped a bone key into the small gap produced by the cut at the back of the head and twisted it, popping the calotte from the base. A strong, persistent pull on the sectioned bone separated it from the brain.

Old blood, almost black in color, pooled around the wound. Splintered bone fragments from the skull's inner and outer tables projected toward the brain. The brain already had begun to shrink and change its shape, taking on the consistency of thick gruel. With some effort, Browning managed to remove it from the skull.

"Death is due to extradural hemorrhage on right side of head. Result of blunt instrument trauma of unknown origin on same side of skull. Some bleeding into subbasilar area. That region may also be fractured. Will reexamine radiographs later."

Maggie tried to imagine the velocity required to crack the skull's base from a lateral blow, but Browning's voice interrupted her thoughts.

"Recommend further evaluation by a forensic anthropologist to assist with possible determination of instrument used and number of blows." She looked up, the hint of a smile lifting the corners of her mouth. Maggie was tempted to grin from ear to ear behind her mask but checked the impulse. Browning definitely was coming around.

Finally, Browning cut into the throat area, viewing the trachea and the larynx. Earlier, the lungs had shown no sign of fluid associated with drowning. Neither did the throat region. The victim was dead when she hit the water.

Browning headed for the mouth. "Maggie, do you want me to cut out her teeth for identification?"

"No," Maggie almost shouted. "I prefer that you just give me the entire head. Less invasive. It will have to be removed anyway to evaluate the trauma. I'll do the dental x-rays and then the trauma analysis so there'll be as few cuts as necessary on the skull." She didn't want Browning to cut out the teeth. Pathologists often missed crucial tooth roots when they removed the jaws.

"Done," Browning said. "Just let me see if there are any dental fillings." Prying open the mouth and holding the thickened tongue to the side with her hemostats, Browning noted, "Good dental health, at least two amalgam fillings in the left lower jaw."

Almost two hours into the autopsy and the only words spoken had been those of Browning and Maggie. An older detective stepped forward.

"Dr. Browning, can you give us an estimate of time since death? We need that information to look for missing persons." Browning's forehead wrinkled into a frown. Her eyes narrowed. Pathologists don't like questions during autopsy. She answered curtly.

"Judging by the condition of the organs and time of year, one, maybe two days." Laying down her tools, she sighed, "Maggie, I'm done. Do you need anything else besides the head?"

"Yep, one more thing," Maggie replied. Even she hated to make Browning's day any longer. "Could you cut out the pubic bones so I can pinpoint the age a little closer? It might help us with the I.D." Maggie really wanted a whole hip bone so she could also look at the auricular surface, the joint that articulates with the sacrum. The best aging tools for adults were the pubic symphysis and the auricular surface, but she knew that removing a hip bone would take more than a few minutes. Browning did not seem to be in the mood.

Browning took her scalpel and quickly removed the tissue surrounding the posterior and inferior portions of the pubic bones. Then, once again, she picked up the autopsy saw and cut through both hip bones, excising the pubes and a small section of each ischium, the bones humans sit on. "Well, that's that," she said. Maggie cleared her throat. They shared a glance, and Browning announced to the other observers, "Autopsy's over, boys."

No sooner had Browning said that than the detectives moved toward the door en masse and quickly slid into the hall, heading toward the light and fresh air. Only one crime scene technician remained behind for fingerprinting after autopsy. "O.K. Maggie" Browning said.

"Let's find a tattoo, Doc," Maggie responded.

"Let's do it," Browning answered back.

Browning began with the hands. Starting with the left and then moving to the right, she checked the skin between all of the fingers for the second time. Nothing. She then looked at the feet, examining them closely, spreading apart the toes one by one, skimming their water-wrinkled surfaces. Next, she searched behind the knees, carefully extending the legs to view the small, darkened creases. She returned to the upper body. She lifted the left arm and looked into its pit, the smooth-shaven, unmarred appearance attesting to the conscientious personal hygiene of the victim. Nothing there.

Maggie motioned for her to lift the right arm. Raising it high above the woman's head and rolling it out and away from the body, they both spotted it at the same time. "Well, I'll be damned, Maggie. There it is."

A small dark tattoo, a little larger than a pencil eraser peered back at them, almost hidden in the folds of skin. A closer look confirmed that it was a circle, a triangle in its center. Maggie gave Browning a questioning look. She shrugged. Cutting the tissue surrounding the tattoo, Browning removed the small section of skin and placed it in a Petri dish.

"Maggie, what does this mean? Why are all of these young women being killed? It must not be sexual assault. The three with soft tissue showed no evidence of that. Yet three of the four victims were killed by what appears to be a single blow to the head. And what about these tattoos? Did they belong to a club or something? We need help here. Can you meet me in my office this evening around six to talk?"

"Sure," Maggie answered.

"I'll call Dan and the lead detective," Browning said. She returned to the body, slicing through the remaining discolored throat tissue with her scalpel, well below the region of the hyoid. Working toward the back of the neck, she quickly exposed the cervical vertebrae with the blade. She placed a skull block beneath the back of the head. When she had the angle just right, she picked up the bone saw. Hesitating only to adjust her position, she cut straight through the fourth and fifth vertebrae. She handed Maggie the head. Without another word, she stripped her gloves from her hands, threw them in the cart marked "biohazard", and walked out the door.

Maggie placed the head in an evidence bag, sealed it, and scribbled her initials across the seal. When she first began her job at the coroner's office, she had found it difficult to request a person's head. Some people, usually family members, were offended by removal of body parts for identification and trauma analysis, especially the head. Often, their concern was based on the memory of what their loved ones looked like the last time they saw them. But the decay process was a wicked thing. Under some circumstances, within twenty-four hours after death a normal face could change into an inscrutable mask, obscuring vital identification and trauma information. Two or three more days and all facial tissue could be destroyed, leaving a skull attached to the rest of the body by just a few decaying tissue strands. When Maggie explained this to grieving family members, they understood the need to carefully examine the bone. Her files were filled with cases where osteological analysis played a pivotal role in the murder trials, more often than not in favor of the prosecution. Those same files were filled with disagreements over final disposition of remains. She encouraged retention of all damaged bones until the fate of the perpetrator had been sealed. Not everyone agreed.

Maggie took the head and the pubic bones down the hall to her lab. She opened the refrigerator door emblazoned with orange and black biohazard signs, then set the two bags on the top shelf. She mentally catalogued the cooler's contents: the new items; two large bags holding the bathtub women's sparse remains; a single human foot that had washed up on the Mississippi River bank a few weeks prior, still encased in its work boot; a couple of dismembered hands found across town in the tub of a Laundromat washing machine; and a deer femur a hunter had turned in to the local sheriff's office. She gave the door a strong, solid push. It closed with a swish. Flipping open the cooler's logbook, she duly noted the new case, chiding herself because she would be getting behind in her analyses. Once behind, it was hard to catch up.

Fresh air and a shower were what she needed. Time to think about the similarities in all the cases. Something more than coffee to temporarily wash death from her mind. She locked her lab, headed down the corridor, and stepped out into the early afternoon. A flash of light momentarily stunned her. Blinking away the spots before her eyes, she almost ran into Rodney Durham and his photographer and crew. "Maggie, any comment about the canal case?" he said, as he thrust the mike into her face.

She stared at him, unsmiling. Then, she shook her head and moved toward her car. She wanted to say, "You arrogant little weasel. Get the hell out of my way." He followed behind her, like an ill wind, lifting the hairs on the back of her neck. When she opened her car door and sat down, the humidity hit her with its suffocating force. It was so thick she could almost touch it. The clouds were rolling in. A storm was coming. It wasn't the only storm on the horizon. She turned toward Rodney Durham, dismissing him with a look. He stared back at her, an inscrutable smile tugging at the corners of his mouth. Maggie could not figure him out. Did he think he knew something about her that he wanted to include in some film or was he just interested in her as an ancillary arm of the coroner's office? She looked at him in her rearview mirror as she started her car. She gunned it a little too much and bounced over the curb. He continued standing near the edge of the street watching her while she put two blocks between them in a matter of seconds.

Chapter 4

Maggie pulled into her building, parking the car in its usual place. Brutus came bounding down the stairs. He almost knocked her over, his typical greeting on the rare occasion she stopped by home in the middle of the day. His enthusiasm could leave her bruised and on her behind if she didn't plant herself firmly before he reached her. Tango lingered at the top of the stairs, his tail moving back and forth with the exactness of a metronome. She gave Brutus a brief hello hug, then hurried up the stairs. Tango scooted away. Brutus quickly followed her, his nose making loud snorting noises as he assessed the death smells clinging to her scrubs. The blinking red light on her answering machine signaled that she had two messages. The first one was from Rodney Durham. "Maggie, I'd like to schedule a meeting with you in your home and do a photo shoot. Call me please."

"A photo shoot. 'Shoot' might be the key word here," she thought. Obviously, he was out of his mind if he thought she was letting him into her home. What was it going to take to get rid of him? She had a sinking feeling in the pit of her stomach as ancient memories tried to surface. She pushed them from her mind and waited for the second message. It was from Eduardo.

"Maggie, the job is yours. I'm sending you photos in a JPEG file. We have all the equipment you need here. Send your point man immediately. I'll meet him Thursday at noon between the monuments in Piazza San Marco, but I need you here without fail within three days. Any problems with this, call me. Otherwise, congratulations and *ciao*!"

"Oh hell," Maggie thought. "What am I going to do? What if another body pops up? Besides, there's something about these tattoos and these cases that doesn't make sense. I have to take care of them before I leave. I owe Dan that much. I just can't go yet. Oh, please, please, Lucas, be sober today. I need your mapping hand to be steady and true."

Maggie wanted to shower before calling Lucas, the pulsating stream of hot water always a calming force. She walked into the bathroom, closed the door, and turned on the water. She removed her scrubs and stepped into the tub. A quick shampoo and an even faster shower. Though she wanted to linger, she had no time. She dried with an old, soft, white towel, temporarily distracted by the holes that were beginning to appear in the thread-weary fabric. Brutus whined at the bathroom door, trying to get closer to her death-filled clothing in a heap on the floor. Only bleach would dissolve his interest in the scrubs.

With renewed vigor, Maggie wrapped the towel around herself and walked into the living room, combing her hair as she went. She dialed Lucas's number. He answered on the third ring.

"Lucas, it's a go. We're in. Did you pass your physical?"

"With flying colors, Maggie."

"Great. Get packed. Call the airline and get a ticket. You're leaving tomorrow for Venice. I hope your passport's valid."

"Yeah, sure it is, Maggie. Gee, this is fast."

"Yep, but you know I told you it would be. Are you O.K. with this?"

"I'm fine."

"Well, here's the deal. You know sort of what Eduardo looks like. You have the old picture of him that I e-mailed you, right?"

"Yeah."

"Well, he'll meet you between the two giant columns in San Marcos Square on Thursday at noon. Remember that the time changes. Let's see, London is six hours ahead of us. Venice is another hour or two ahead of that. Oh, well, look it up! What will you do for an assistant to help you with the mapping?"

"Maggie, I can handle this. I'm not a child. Just relax. When are you coming?"

"I'll be there in one or two days, I hope. Lucas, do not remove a single bone until I get there."

"I believe we've done this before, Maggie. I know your rules. Map and hold. If I finish mapping before you get there, I'll just start reviewing the history of the place, or whatever Eduardo has for us. And, Maggie?" He paused. "I wanted you to know that I have not had a single drink since your first call."

"Lucas, that's great," she replied sincerely. "I'm proud of you. Welcome back. Oh, by the way, I need some names of local tattoo shops, and where did you get those god-awful ones that you *will* keep covered in Venice?"

"My tattoos? That's a long story. I'll tell you another time. I have to get packed now, but there are tattoo shops all over the place these days. Two or three good ones are out in Metairie, but there's also one in the Quarter. Been there a long time, The Red Parrot near Toulouse and North Rampart. You want to tell me what you're up to?"

"Later."

"O.K. See you in a gondola in a few days. Take care, Maggie. Watch out for those tattoo artists. They can talk you into the darndest things, but you already know that. Anyway, gotta go. What's that Italian saying, Hi-ho."

"Very funny, everyone's a comedian these days. It's *ciao.*"

"Oh well, whatever works. And, Maggie . . ."

"Yeah?"

"Thank you."

"For what?"

"I believe you know."

"See you, my friend," Maggie said as she hung up the phone. She felt relieved after talking with Lucas. He seemed to be on track again. The shower had rejuvenated her so she dressed quickly. On the way out the door, she grabbed a Coke from the fridge rather than a glass of the merlot she had set out earlier. She headed back to the lab. She wanted to go over all four cases again before she met with Browning and Dan. She wanted to find something she'd missed. She needed to be ready for the next one, if it came, and she had no reason to assume it would not.

The morgue was locked tight. Maggie opened the outside door and headed down the hall to her lab. The doors to the autopsy rooms were ajar. Everyone must have left early. She unlocked her lab and turned on the light. Starting on the new Jane Doe now would help her finish sooner tomorrow. She pulled a box of gloves from the drawer, set out several new scalpel blades, and grabbed a disposable face mask from the shelf above her desk. Browning's assistant had already x-rayed the entire body, so she could move straight into the second phase of her work, complete maceration of the skull. She opened the refrigerator and took out the bag with the skull in it. After sitting down at the stainless steel analysis table, she slowly pulled the parts of the skull from the bag. She looked into what was left of the sightless eyes, hoping for a brief glimpse into the mystery of who the victim was. Maggie had trained her mind over the years to separate the bones from the victim. Some cases were easier than others. By its very nature, the autopsy had rendered the skull less human. By accepting that, she could continue to process the bone without thinking too much about what it had been. The little tissue that was left inside the cranium clung to its walls tenaciously.

Picking up the Rongeurs, a fancy name for pliers that added a hundred bucks to their price, she carefully began to remove as much of the periosteum as possible. On the external surface of the skull, she cut away the masseter, buccinator, and temporalis muscles. The tenacious tissue would require soaking in detergent water and even heating for a few hours to speed up the tissue removal and to make it easier to dissect out the hyoid.

Looking more closely at the two wedges of the right temporal bone that had been fractured by the head trauma, Maggie jotted down notes describing how bone fragments extended medially into the inner vault region.

Laying down her pencil, she became fixated on the skull's warped appearance. Once again, she was drawn to the skull as representing a victim, not just some bones. As she examined the splintered bone that had been driven into the brain, she couldn't help but remember an article she had read recently in some psychology journal. Though the article seemed a little far fetched, it suggested that the brain might be the last organ to actually shut down at death, fading slowly till the light became less and less discernible. In the moments of her last light, had the victim seen the one who did this to her? Had the watery brain tissue that the pathologist dumped into the biohazard bag carried not only the knowledge of what had hit the young woman but the identity of her killer?

With her back toward the door and concentrating on the skull, Maggie didn't hear Sidney enter the room. She almost dropped her scalpel when he spoke.

"Miss Maggie, you O.K.? You look kind of green."

"Good God, Sidney," she said, turning toward him. "I didn't realize my door was unlocked. I never heard you open it. You scared the hell out of me."

"I didn't mean to scare you." There was a slight but noticeable catch in his voice.

Maggie softened her reply. "Well, it's O.K. *this* time, but where is everyone?"

Regaining his composure, Sidney replied, "Doc's gone for the day, something about her allergy problems. She said to tell you she'd talk to you tomorrow about these cases. I just came back to close up and set the alarm. If you're gonna be here a while, would you set the alarm when you leave?"

"O.K. By the way, how are your headaches these days? Are you still having them?"

"What? Oh. Yeah. Once in a while. Some kind of

syndrome they say. I think it's the war."

"The war? Desert Storm?"

"No, Vietnam."

"Vietnam? I didn't realize you were old enough to have gone there."

"Barely. I just turned 18 when I volunteered. They gave me bag duty."

"What's that?"

"Puttin' soldiers into body bags and loading 'em onto the choppers to send them home."

"Sidney, that's awful. Maybe a morgue isn't the place for you to be working these days."

"That's funny, Miss Maggie. No disrespect, but look at you. You got somebody's head in your hands."

"Yeah, I guess you're right," Maggie said, glancing at the partially cleaned skull. "Maybe we both need our own heads examined. Do me a favor, though. Check out those headaches again, would you? If nothing else, get another opinion."

"Oh, O.K."

Sidney backed out the door. She couldn't hear his footsteps, but she heard the outer door bang shut. She walked over to her door and closed it, flipping the dead-bolt from the inside.

She sat down at her desk again. She used a magnifying glass to focus on small pieces of grainy orange and white material that were embedded in the scalp and the bone. Some of the material was also stuck to blood-matted strands of hair that had been pushed into the inner vault by the force of the blow. Tile? Brick? According to Browning, none of the other victims had anything in the scalp tissue. Maggie collected the fine, powdery material and placed it in a paper envelope. Maybe the trace evidence people could identify it.

Turning over the skull and glancing at its base, she noticed the vertebrae were still attached and the hyoid was in place. "The hyoid sits just below the tongue and anchors muscles in place that aid in speech," she said to herself. Maggie often was inclined to recite anatomical tidbits to herself as she separated individuals bone by bone, bit by bit. She left the vertebrae and hyoid attached to the rest of the skull. Hot water would separate the tissue from the bone, and then she could look for a fracture around and near the foramen magnum, the large opening in the base of the skull. A fracture to the base didn't necessarily mean that someone got struck there. Because it has so many small openings for nerves and vessels and the one big one through which the spinal chord passes, the base of the skull is particularly vulnerable to trauma from a variety of head injuries. In one of Maggie's cases, the force from a blow to the jaw had cracked the base of the victim's skull.

Placing the skull in a pot on the hot plate, she added water and detergent, turning the temperature to high. Then she took the bag with the fragile pubic bones from the refrigerator, cut the excess tissue from them and tied them in knee-high panty hose. She added them to the pot. Knee-highs were great for keeping small things from getting lost. They also eliminated the task of trying to figure out what side of the body some of the hand and foot bones belonged to if you were working on a whole body. Left hand in one stocking, right hand in another. Same for the feet. The hot water and detergent didn't harm the cheap knee-highs.

When she pulled a chair up to the analysis table and sat down, Maggie noticed that the folder she had hurriedly made for the new case earlier that day lay next to the ones for the other three. "Funny," she mused, "I thought I put these files in the cabinet yesterday. I guess I left them out."

She laid out all four files in a row and began to remove the contents of the first three, one analysis card at a time. She felt as though she were playing solitaire as she placed each form below the other with its file folder at the top of the row. She made a new set of cards for victim number four and then began to study them all.

Victim #1	Victim #2	Victim #3	Victim #4
Brown	Doe 1	Martin	Doe 2
Black	Black	White	Black
age: 25	21-27	25	Under 30
No trauma	Trauma	Trauma	Trauma
Drugs	No drugs	No drugs	Drugs (?)
No skin	Tattoo	Tattoo	Tattoo
Nude	Clothed	Clothed	Clothed
Address (?)	Address (?)	Mid City	Address (?)

Obviously, the first victim wasn't exactly like the other three. The latest three had head trauma, but no apparent sexual trauma. The stage of decomposition of the first victim left investigators unable to rule out drowning or sexual assault, but she had no head trauma. Maggie looked at her name on the file. Dorothy Brown. Dorothy did not have head trauma, but she did have something else the other women did not have, that cinder block tied to her leg, the knot in the rope securing it looking suspiciously nautical. The other victims were free floaters.

All four women were young. Dorothy was a prostitute. The other woman who had been identified, Betty Martin, was an accountant. How upstanding could you get? The occupation of the two remaining victims was unknown, at least for now. Maggie knew she had to get them identified before she could begin to figure out background similarities, if they existed. She might even have to reconstruct their faces in clay or try a computer enhancement to see if anyone could recognize them— tasks she couldn't perform until she returned from Venice.

Were these deaths the work of a serial killer? All she had ever read by the big-name profilers indicated that sexual assault or, at the very least, torture of some kind was often associated with serial killing. Just how did he manage to catch these three young women unaware without a struggle? Could someone realistically just sneak up on them and hit them over the head like that? She thought of Sidney and how he had just scared the daylights out of her without even trying when he had silently entered the lab behind her.

One thing was certain, no attempt had been made to hide the last three bodies. After Dorothy Brown surfaced, the killer knew the other ones would do the same unless he attached something heavier than a cinder block to them. Following that failed attempt, the killer must have wanted the other bodies to be found, or maybe he was just in a hurry. Something wasn't right. Someone had blood on his hands and all the perfume of Arabia wouldn't sweeten them. There had to be an explanation, and closet detective or not, Margaret Rose Andrepont wanted to find it.

Maybe a city map might help. How close were the dump sites to one another? Though the water probably transported the bodies, it might not have moved them out of the general vicinity where they had first entered the canals. She was certain the detectives had already checked that out, but she wanted to see for herself.

She decided to take a ride even though a storm was coming. The new case could wait until tomorrow.

Besides, soaking the head overnight in detergent would make her job easier. She placed the analysis cards back in their folders and put all of the files under her arm. Something might come to her later.

Maggie turned off the hot plate, unplugged its cord, flipped the light switch, and left the lab. Pulling on her office door to make sure it had locked, she took a few steps. Then, distracted by her thoughts, she turned back to check the door again. Quickly, she headed toward the exit, where the green light on the alarm system key pad reminded her to set the alarm. She punched in the code and pressed the "arm" button. "Arm, disarm, body references everywhere," she thought. But she liked the new security system, even though she had never known anyone to try to break into the morgue. "Has anyone ever tried to break out?" she thought. "Oh, great, I'm turning into Jimmy O'Malley, news sleuth for all of New Orleans."

Maggie's car had a parking ticket beneath the wiper blade. Someone had written her a brief message.

"Maggie, next time this will be real. We're getting complaints from pedestrians."

She slipped the ticket into her pocket. She was saving them. She had almost enough to paper one wall of her bathroom.

Maggie laid the case files on the passenger seat and pulled out her city map. After putting a small red dot where each of the four victims had been found, she couldn't see any pattern. She wanted to drive past the scenes anyway.

Just as she started her car, the rain began—small drops, then larger ones. If it continued, the streets would flood. New Orleans was below sea level, and it flooded on a regular basis. She could just see her car stalling in the middle of some busy intersection. She didn't want to risk getting rear-ended by a careless driver. She could grab a city bus to the Quarter and check out the Red Parrot instead. Maggie drove to the back of the morgue parking lot, locked the doors of the Karmann Ghia, and walked to the corner bus stop.

There was standing room only on the bus. Maggie got off the bus after a few blocks and walked toward Canal Street and the Quarter. The rain had turned to a drizzle, and the shower had done nothing to discourage the tourists. Wading into their midst, she made her way along several blocks, taking a left on Royal, where antique shops with staggering prices lined the street. The only thing close to an antique that she owned was an old bow-front chest she had found in a shop in Ponchatoula, twenty or so miles north of New Orleans. Maggie hesitated long enough at one shop to admire a French clock on an equally French sideboard, then continued on her way. She went one more block and turned north on Toulouse. She walked slowly down the street until she saw the shop.

Sandwiched in among the other shops was a fading, hand-painted sign with a red parrot on it. It looked like all the other storefronts up and down the street. The giveaway was the scrubbed-clean, intense young woman standing near the entrance. She was studying something on the top of her arm. From what Maggie could see as she got closer, it was a tattoo, a blazing sun with vine-like rays projecting from it, wrapping themselves around her forearm and extending toward her fingers. Maggie wondered how cool that would look in a courtroom if the woman ever decided on a legal career. She guessed the woman would be hard pressed to convince a jury of someone's innocence or guilt if they caught sight of her own street markings. It wasn't that Maggie disliked tattoos. In fact, she kind of liked them. It was the need for some people to cover a major part of their body with them that she found curious. She understood too well how permanent tattoos were. The girl didn't acknowledge Maggie's presence as Maggie slipped past her into the brightly lit shop.

Immediately, she heard the distinctive, high-pitched, staccato buzz of the needle as it penetrated someone's skin at a phenomenal speed, piercing hundreds of holes per minute in the dermal layer, drilling miniature wells into which the colored ink flowed like water.

A beaded doorway separated the outer shop from the source of the sound. The young man behind the front counter looked up from his reading, standing his book on end. A copy of *Moby Dick* rested in his hand. Maggie caught a glimpse of a silver post in his tongue as he quickly licked his bottom lip. She was struck by the fact that he she saw no tattoos on him—that is, until he turned to place his book on a shelf behind him. The tentacles of an octopus or a squid radiated from beneath his T-shirt, curled up his neck and down the back of his arms to just below the elbows.

"Can I help you, lady?" he said as he turned toward her, following her eyes with amusement.

"Do you do tattoos?" Maggie answered.

"Not me. She does," he said, tossing his head toward the beaded doorway.

"She?" Maggie's memory of sailors and the hairy men who tattooed them took a dive.

"Yeah, you want one?"

"No. I just want some information about tattoos. Do you think I could ask her?"

"Probably, if you wanna wait. She'll take a break in a while. She's doing a hard one, and you can't go back there."

"I'll wait."

He returned to his book. Maggie quickly scanned the patterns covering the walls. Everything from cartoon characters to nautical symbols to flowers and insects filled the shop. One whole section was dedicated to Celtic symbols, a hot item with younger clients. She saw nothing even close to the simple patterns they had found on the murder victims. Maggie had been in the shop for almost an hour and was about to leave when she heard the rattle of beads as a young man came out of the back room. He looked ill and walked very slowly toward the exit. She wondered what had just been etched on his body and where. The clerk disappeared behind the beads and returned a few minutes later.

"Dahlia will be out in a little bit."

"Thanks."

Moments later the beads parted again and a striking, tall brunette with vacant, liquid-blue eyes walked toward Maggie. She moved with confidence and could have been a model in another life. She looked familiar.

"You got five minutes," she said.

"My name is Maggie Andrepont and I just wanted your opinion on some tattoos."

"Why me?"

"Lucas Evans said you might help."

"Lucas?" Her eyes softened for a moment. Then Maggie realized why she looked familiar. She was the woman with Lucas that night at Mother's Restaurant. Sober, she looked different.

A little impatient, Dahlia said, "Well . . ."

Maggie blurted out, "Symbols, monochromatic, small circles with wavy lines, triangles, lightening rods in them. Sound familiar to you?"

"No, not really. How small?"

"About the size of the end of your little finger or a pencil eraser."

"Hm."

"Also, do you do tattoos in odd places?"

"Lady, I do tattoos in *all* places. What do you mean 'odd places'?"

"Under the arms, between the toes."

"Not usually. Those areas are too tender. It hurts like hell."

"That's what I thought. Thanks."

"No problem. By the way, where is Lucas these days?"

"On his way to Venice, Italy, tomorrow."

"Really?" Her lowered eyes gave away her disappointment.

"Thanks, Dahlia. If I have more questions, could I come back to talk with you?"

"I guess," she said, her eyes once again impenetrable. Turning abruptly, she walked toward the beaded doorway, a slight change in the way she carried herself. The beads swung wildly when she pushed them aside and disappeared.

As Maggie left the shop, a middle-aged, conservatively-dressed man entered. The wedding band on his left ring finger elicited an unreturned grin from her as she wondered how he might decorate his body. She was tired and walked toward Poydras to catch a bus back to the lab. Enough sleuthing for one day.

Maggie got off the bus near the morgue and hurried toward the parking lot at the back of the building. She would be glad to get home. The Ghia was the only car left in the lot. As she neared the car, she realized the new top had been cut from side to side near where it connected to the windshield. Her heart began to thump against her chest with each step she took. A tightness in the back of her neck brought with it a slight chill. She quickly looked around the lot, unlocked the driver's side door, and jumped in locking the door. Once she felt a little safer inside, it sunk in. "Damn. Damn. Damn. What slithering piece of manure did this?" she shouted.

The lot was enclosed on three sides. You could not get there without walking along the side of the building. Only as you rounded the corner would you have seen her car. Someone had to have walked that way deliberately. Had she hacked off somebody that much, or was it simply a thief? Thinking of the money she had just spent on the top, she felt sick. Guess she would just wait until tomorrow to report it. It wouldn't do any good anyway. They would never find out who was responsible. Calming down a little, her hands shaking, she looked around inside. Nothing seemed to be disturbed. The stack of files still lay on the passenger seat, a little damp, but unhurt. More relieved, she thought, "Too bad they didn't steal my cell phone."

She became aggravated again as she pulled out of the lot. She darted through a couple of yellow lights down the street and one that was turning red. She was driving like a typical New Orleanian who viewed the yellow light as the pacing flag at the Indianapolis 500, but she decided she had better be careful at the traffic lights. The traffic cameras were everywhere these days. She took a deep breath and slowed down. It wasn't as though she hadn't considered that something could happen to the new top, but she had at least hoped to have it for a little while before it did. Something stronger than aggravation entered her mind, but she wouldn't acknowledge the growing apprehension. Instead, she focused on the anger that came with being Irish.

"Damn. Damn. Damn."

She drove the rest of the way home in silence, thinking of the bottle of merlot she had waiting on the kitchen counter. It was definitely a three-glass night.

Maggie pressed the remote and the garage door opened. As she pulled inside, Moses walked in from the courtyard. He could see by the look on her face that she was in a mood.

"Miss Maggie, I'm headed home now. I planted some marigolds and zinnias like your mama loved in the iron pots by the front gate. I also planted verbena by that old rusted iron fence post you brought home last month."

Distantly, she answered, "What? Oh, O.K. Moses. Thanks for what you did today."

Brutus came bounding down the stairs just as she started to tell Moses about the car. He couldn't decide which of them to lick first and turned in circles from Moses to Maggie, his huge tail slapping both of them as he went. Maggie lost her footing and slid onto the floor, laughing, almost hysterically, until even Brutus stopped jumping about. Her frustration with the events of the day was taking its obvious toll.

Moses just looked at her for a long moment and walked out the door.

Chapter 5

Maggie's cell phone almost danced across her bedside table around 9 p.m., just as she was about to pick up the stack of case files and go over them again. She took the last sip from her second glass of wine and checked the caller. Dan. "Oh, no," she said out loud. "Please don't let it be a bad coroner's case this late at night." She answered with a reserved "hello."

"Maggie, you're not going to believe this."

"Not another one in the canals?"

"I'm not sure. It's only a piece of a skull, but can I send it over? It's clean and doesn't smell."

"Oh, why not? Nothing's sacred anymore, much less my simple abode. Who's bringing it?"

"Someone from Fifth District. It was found at the edge of one of the canals over their way."

Maggie was beginning to feel like a bungee jumper, permanently attached to Dan at one end, but dangling like a puppet with nothing to grab. Something had to give if she was ever going to get to Venice.

The young officer rang Maggie's doorbell, standing at attention after she ushered him onto the first-floor landing. Brutus sniffed him up and down, declared him harmless, then went on his way. Tango sat midway up the stairs, not budging. Maggie stood near the door, broke the police seal on the brown paper bag, and opened it, ready to add another case to her growing list of canal victims.

She felt immediate relief as she pulled the skull from the bag. It was human all right, but this soul had not seen the light of day in at least a hundred years. Some of the facial bones were still intact, and the thick brow ridges, narrow nasal opening, and oval eye orbits clearly indicated that it was a white male. But it was the teeth that told her what she needed to know. They were heavily worn on their biting surface, a condition not seen in modern populations with refined sugar diets. The secondary dentin that formed after the enamel had worn away gave the teeth a yellowish cast. The bone was dark brown, an indication that it had been buried for quite a long time, long enough for its porous surface to take on the color of the soil around it. It must have washed up from the bottom of the canal. "Maybe I hold the head of one of my Irish ancestors in my hands," Maggie thought, as she carefully returned the cranium to the bag and sent the policeman on his way. She called Dan. "We're lucky this time," she told him. "It's a male who died a hundred or more years ago. I'll follow up on it tomorrow, but it has nothing to do with the bodies in the canals."

"Well, thank God for that, Maggie," the relief obvious in his voice.

"Dan, I need to get to Venice," Maggie responded wearily. "This affects my entire future. You know we have discussed how important this historic project is to me."

"O.K., Maggie, I understand. But let's meet one more time tomorrow. If nothing new comes in by then, I don't know why a few days in Venice would change anything around here."

"Fine. Tomorrow I'll work as late as I have to on the new Jane Doe, even if it's all night, but I'm making reservations to fly to Venice Friday morning. Do you hear me, Dan? Friday morning."

"Guess I can't think of anything else to keep you here, but could you please leave a telephone number where you can be reached in Venice in case I need you?"

"Yes, but you'd better not call me there unless it's to report your own death."

"Maggie, sometimes I think you're not kidding."

Maggie hung up with a brief goodbye. She thought about Dan for a while. Surely he knew she was kidding. Why couldn't she let anybody get close to her? Some days she was so scared about her future: a woman, alone. Maybe it was fear of rejection, of never measuring up, as her father had always implied. Though a tomboy since youth, she was not the son he had wanted all those years ago. When he blamed her mother for Maggie's being a girl, Maggie shouldn't have told him what she had learned in biology class, that the male determined the sex of his offspring. She still carried the small scar on her chin from that one. Sometimes she hid her deepest pain with her acerbic sense of humor.

She started to pour another glass of merlot and decided against it. Two were her usual limit. The memory of her father's habitual drunkenness, the beatings that came with it, often made her wonder why she drank even one or two glasses of wine. She crawled back into bed and pushed the files aside. She tried to clear everything from her mind, but Rodney Durham's face popped up and with it the little she actually knew about him. He had made a few documentaries on New Orleans and had received some attention for a couple of them, one on corruption in local law enforcement, the other on the public school system. Though both had received decent reviews, they had not won him any friends. What was his angle with her? She began to drift.

She awoke some time later, in the middle of the night. Tango's tail was in her face. Brutus' body was cutting off the circulation in her left leg, and he was growling. Something wasn't right. Something had awakened him. Brutus bolted from the bedroom and raced down the stairs. Maggie was right behind Tango, who was practically riding Brutus' tail.

Brutus stood at the front door, his thundering bark loud enough to dislodge the dead. After looking through the peephole and seeing nothing, Maggie slowly opened the door and took a step outside. All she could see were a few shadows cast by the dim streetlight on the corner. She stepped back inside and turned to close the door. As she did, her hand touched a roughened area near the lock on the outer side of the door. A closer look revealed fresh, deep scratches and grooves in the wood near the lock. Someone had been working on the lock, trying to break it. It must have been a stranger, unaware that she had a 165-pound man-eater as a doorman. "Just what is going on?" she thought. A call to the police would accomplish nothing at this hour. Whoever had done it was probably long gone.

Maggie made sure the lock was secure and tried to laugh as she headed back up the stairs, thinking of Brutus' greeting to any would-be intruder. At the same time, that dark something nagged at her. Who would want to enter her house at this time of night, knowing full well that, most likely, she would be at home? "Tomorrow I think I will call the alarm company to check out their prices for a building like mine," she mouthed out loud.

She took her mother's old .38 out of the dresser drawer, removed the trigger lock, and gingerly laid the gun on her bedside table. She didn't like guns. Her work had shown her all too well what they could do to a human being. Hopping back into bed and pulling the top sheet up to her chin, she called to Brutus and Tango. They both jumped onto the bed at the same time, almost throwing her off the other side.

Chapter 6

N o one was around when Maggie got to the morgue the next morning, not even Sidney, though she figured the investigator only came in before 8 a.m. for special cases. Six thirty was too early even for him. She had to finish the new case so she could leave for Venice. She opened the outside door and was caught off guard by the security system's warning. Still a little wary of the thing, she quickly punched in the code and waited for the beep and green light that indicated the system was disarmed.

Thank goodness the head was still where she had left it, in the pot on top of the burner. "But where else would it have been?" she chided herself. She decided she truly was getting paranoid. She drained the water from the pot, turning her head slightly to prevent the pungent odor from rising directly into her nose. She added clean water and detergent and set the heat on high. A little more time and the tenacious tissue would just fall away. She sat down at her desk and began to go through the victims' files. She counted them. Only three files were in the stack. Now where was the other file? Which one was missing? Dorothy Brown's. She looked on the floor near the desk and then realized Dorothy's file must have slid behind the headboard at home when she got the call from Dan about the skull from Fifth District. After the young officer left, she never picked up the files again. Heaven only knows where Dorothy Brown's file landed after the would-be intruder situation. She could look for it when she got home. It was probably under her bed with a herd of dust bunnies. For now, she needed to finish the new canal case.

The pubic bones were still in the water, and Maggie fished around in the pot with a pair of tongs, trying to grab the knee-high stockings in which she had tied them. She untied the stockings and looked at the pubes, relieved she had remembered them. But the pantyhose brought the case home again to Maggie and distracted her from her immediate task. She thought about how the young woman would never again dress up for a special occasion, never again walk barefoot through a field of clover, never again try on a new pair of shoes. She willed herself back to being analytical.

A little cartilage clung to the symphyseal faces of the pubes here and there. She had to get them clean and dried, or the soft, spongy bones would disintegrate, leaving her right back where she started from with only a rough age estimate for the new Jane Doe. Age estimation could be extremely important in getting her identified. Maggie rinsed the water from the bones, gently teased the remaining cartilage from their edges, and placed them on a tray beneath the fume hood to dry. A light knock on her door made her jump.

"Maggie?"

"Yeah! Come in." Yancy Berthelot, the chemist down the hall, tentatively opened the door. She had stuck a note on his door asking him to stop by when he got to work. He eased the door open just another inch or two, and Maggie motioned for him to enter. The trace evidence people never liked to come into her lab. The sights and smells were not for the squeamish.

"It's O.K., Yancy," she said with a grin. "Not much going on today that will interfere with your lunch."

"What's up, Maggie?"

"I have what looks like some kind of grainy powder that was embedded in the hair and scalp of the new canal case. There's not much of it, but could you look at it for me?"

"Sure. I'll have a look and try to get back to you in a few days. By the way, I heard you're headed for deep waters in a day or so."

"You might say that. I'm going to Venice."

"Venice, Louisiana?"

"I'm surrounded by comedians these days, but that's a pretty good comeback, especially since our Venice has lots of water around it, too. But, you know I mean Venice, Italy. The word has gotten around. You want to go with me? I could use a good chemist."

"Are you paying my way?"

"I wish I could, Yancy, but you know how funding is in this business."

"Just kidding."

"Hey, though, I might have a small consulting job for you on the Venice project when I get back if there's trace evidence to analyze. Are you interested?"

"Sure, just holler. See ya." He backed out the door, having come only close enough to Maggie's desk to take the evidence from her hand. His body was in constant motion as he quickly exited what he and the other technicians called "Beelzebub's kitchen."

Maggie turned back to her work on the skull, separating out the hyoid and trimming the last tissue away from its fragile surfaces. It was undamaged, the center portion, or body, and horns on each side of it unfused, not broken.

She was removing the last of the cartilage when the phone rang. Reluctantly, she picked it up and answered with a curt hello.

"Maggie, I know you are working on the canal cases. Can I interview you?" Rodney Durham blurted out.

"Rodney, I cannot tell you a single thing about these cases. You know that." She snapped icily.

"That's O.K. I just wanted to get some action shots to follow up on those I got at the canal."

"You were at the canal?"

"Yeah. I arrived just as you were unzipping the bag. You looked so serious. Great shots."

"You little worm," she thought. Out loud she said, "Forget it. I will not contribute to your trying to sensationalize these women's cases." Maggie thought she heard some expletive as she hung up the phone. She returned to the skull.

She had almost finished removing the last of the tissue from the skull when the coroner stuck his head in the doorway. "Hi, Maggie. How you doing today?"

"Hello, Dan," she answered cautiously, expecting a lot more than just "how you doing" to bring him down to the lab in the bowels of the building.

"I have a little something else for you to examine when you want to take a break from the new canal case."

"Dan, just show me now. You know I can't stand the suspense."

He pulled a small bag from behind his back and handed it to her. "One of the night owls from the tattoo convention that's in town picked this up on Burgundy Street this morning around 2 a.m. What do you think?"

She was a lot more interested in the fact that a tattoo convention was being held in town than curious about what was in the bag. But she looked inside anyway. The sweet smell of barbecue sauce rose upward, filling her nose. Some movie she had rented about a bad guy who ended up as lunch from the barbecue grill entered her mind, but she certainly didn't want to go there on what she hoped was her last day in town. She pulled the sticky, brown item from the sack with a gloved hand and looked at it. Sharp cuts were evident on several of the bones, but the leftovers from a *cochon de lait* would not keep her stateside this time. "Can you say roasted Porky Pig, Dan?" Even as he smiled, he looked relieved.

"I knew that it didn't look human, Maggie, but I just wanted to be sure."

"What's this about a tattoo convention in town? Why hasn't someone mentioned that to me?"

"It's been all over the TV and in the newspaper, but I guess you haven't had time to check it out. They're meeting over at the Aqua Hotel."

"Dan, would you send someone over there to ask about the tattoos? I just can't do that and finish up here, too."

"Sure, Maggie, I'll send Sidney." Her look stopped him. "Or maybe not."

"Dan, send Yancy or someone else from Trace Evidence. They'll know more about it."

"I'll go myself, Maggie." Noticing her relief, he looked directly into her eyes and quipped, "I haven't seen any tattoos up close in a long time." She gave him a withering look, but he just grinned and ducked out the door. After he left, she knew she should have told him about her late night visitor, but he would have gotten all protective on her. She would not allow herself to appear vulnerable, not this time.

Maggie finished cleaning the skull and examined it. It was warped, an immediate clue that distinguished blunt-force trauma from a gunshot wound. Often, bullets could leave a skull in dozens of pieces that could be reconstructed like a puzzle—neatly, cleanly. Blunt force distorted the skull. Something flat hit the new Jane Doe's head and hit it hard. Maybe Yancy would find a clue as to what in his trace evidence lab. His experience with the smallest bits of material that looked like dust and debris had proven invaluable in the past in solving homicide cases.

The meeting with Browning and Dan to discuss the new canal victim wasn't going to happen. Browning's allergies had sent her to bed. They would just have to wait until after Maggie returned from Venice next week. Hopefully, no new cases would be added to Maggie's growing list of young women from the canals. She also hoped that whoever was screwing with her mind would simply drop out of sight or drop dead.

Chapter 7

Before Maggie left home for the airport to catch her plane to Venice, she wrote a note for Moses. "Hey, Moses. You know the routine. Plenty of food for Brutus and Tango. Back in two or three days. Thanks for everything. By the way, you have not told me lately what I owe you for the garden work you've been doing. Please let me know." She had told Moses earlier about the would-be intruder and knew that he would check on her house as though it were his own. Maggie drove her Karmann Ghia to the airport, the duct tape on the inside of the soft top reminding her to check her rearview mirror more often than usual to see if she was being followed. She definitely needed a vacation.

She boarded the MD80 at Louis Armstrong International Airport and headed down the aisle, passing first class where a few of the occupants were engrossed in whatever business they could quickly pull onto their laps. In the past, first-class passengers typically avoided eye contact with those headed to economy. Even all these years after September 11, many passengers scrutinize everyone else when they board a plane. Maggie felt as though she was walking a gauntlet as she headed down the aisle looking for adequate space in the overhead bin close to her assigned seat. She looked directly at the passengers on both sides of the aisle as she struggled toward the rear of the plane, relieved that she recognized none of them. She found her usual window seat for the short hop to Atlanta and settled in. The takeoff was a little bumpy. It was because of the heat she overheard someone say.

A few minutes into the flight and she'd calmed the barely audible flutter in the pit of her stomach. Her days of white-knuckle flying were finally over. It just happened a few years ago on a flight to Boston for the annual forensics convention. She took a bold step and decided to give up her need to control every situation, a hard thing for her. She finally accepted that pilots probably were not daredevils. They also had families and friends to whom they wished to return safely. She had always found it difficult to let go of the reins and "ride the wild wind," as Jimmy would say. It was scary to think that sometimes Jimmy O'Malley, her goofy friend for life and ace *Picayune* reporter, could be profound.

Out of Atlanta, Maggie's companion in the adjoining bulkhead seat seemed reasonable enough, a retired taxidermist flying to England to study age-old stuffing techniques. His annoyance at her less-than-serious question about whether ancient human trophy heads had been stuffed by the first taxidermists was obvious. He clearly was finished with his attempt at polite conversation, and they both returned to their own thoughts.

Maggie decided to make a list of things to do when she arrived in Venice in order to recover the skeletons in the basement chamber of the campanile as quickly as possible, pack them up, and ship them to America for the analysis. Unfinished work waited for both Lucas and her when they returned home.

The list didn't materialize. She started thinking about the canal victims instead. What was the story there? Who were those women? Where had they come from? Why did only one of them have a weight attached to her? She couldn't forget that they were all so young. Two names were known. Two were not. They all looked healthy. Only one was a druggie. Toxicology had confirmed that. What was the connection to the canals? Quick disposal? Not really. It took some effort to get them there. Most of the canals had fences that separated them from pedestrians. Of course, those fences were full of holes, but why not just drop the women on the street somewhere or in a dark alley? Or maybe by the levee? Had anyone seen what happened? Was more than one person involved? All she had were questions, no answers.

After two bottles of water, two small glasses of wine, and a trip to the restroom, nothing seemed as urgent as before. Maggie flipped up the TV monitor attached to her seat and checked the progress of the flight. Just as she thought, right smack in the middle of the Atlantic. She always seemed to be in the middle of an ocean. She turned it off, closed her eyes, and let the paperback she'd purchased at the airport slip down into the side of her seat. *Something Is Buried in My Back Yard* could wait for another time and so could the other things that were juggling for position in her brain. She briefly saw Dan's face as she settled in for a short nap, a smile playing at the corners of her mouth.

Maggie awoke to the sound of the loudspeaker announcing preparation for landing at Gatwick. She couldn't believe she'd slept so long. The taxidermist was still asleep, his head resting on her shoulder. With a firm push, she heaved him to one side. He finally began to wake up, making funny little clicking sounds with his tongue in the process. He straightened his clothes as the plane's wheels touched the tarmac and the pilot taxied to the gate. When the plane slowed to a stop, he and Maggie gave each other the goodbye nod of indifferent strangers. For a brief moment, Maggie thought of how Rodney Durham's head might look if it were stuck on the end of a pole. She still wondered why he seemed so interested in doing a documentary on her and her work in particular. However, he had not tried to contact her since she practically hung up on him recently. If she were lucky, maybe he had decided to harass someone else.

It was midafternoon before Maggie left Gatwick on a plane to Milan. In Milan, she barely caught the last puddle jumper to Mestre, the small city on the mainland linked to Venice, or "Venezia," as the locals called it. Twilight slipped in seven hours early for her, but she wasn't that sleepy. The "nap" she had gotten on the plane obviously had helped.

She settled into her small hotel, the Dolce, and then grabbed a taxi down to the pier. She wanted to see the lights of Venice across the water. She felt the need to recall that brief but prophetic conversation with Eduardo when she spoke with him by phone on her first trip to Europe five years earlier. That conversation was forever seared into her memory. At the time, he had seemed genuinely excited to hear from her and even more elated to report the recent birth of his first son. Maggie felt stupid to think that he could meet her in Venice that year. They had not actually seen each other since graduate school, and she had no idea at the time that he'd gotten married. Her timing never seemed to be in sync with the men in her life. Should she call him? Maybe.

She realized, however, that she only had an office phone number for him, nothing personal. He would find her at the campanile. That she knew.

Maggie stood on the pier and watched a few boats that were heading toward Venice, but she had no desire to cross the shallow lagoon that evening. She'd heard a little too much about night waters lately. Instead, she looked at Venice from a distance. She remembered the words of her former tour guide from her first trip. The young woman had been so enthusiastic about the history of her island people. Maggie had listened intently as she spoke of the group of 118 small islands that had provided a haven for people who fled Rome and its environs after the empire's collapse and invasion by hordes from the east. The island had always been safe from invaders because of the difficulty of hunting people down in the salt marshes. Many of the fleeing Romans settled there permanently, and by the eighth century Venice had begun to emerge as a maritime nation.

But by the 1700s Venice had changed from a nation of expansion to one of entrenchment. Napoleon brought the maritime giant to its knees and became the first aggressor in almost two thousand years to destroy Venice's independence. This defeat coupled with the ever-increasing problem of the subsidence of the city's limited land surface led Venice into a steady decline.

Only in the latter part of the twentieth century had tourism and foreign investors helped to restore some of the majestic architecture of the lagoon nation. Recently, Venice had become the home of annual film and art festivals that attracted the rich from all over the world. The influx of foreign visitors had helped to draw attention to the deteriorating campanile Maggie had come to investigate. Maggie had not forgotten the sometimes harsh but romantic past of Venice.

The lights of Venice brightened the night sky, pulling Maggie toward it once more, but for some reason unsettling her. Was it her meeting with Eduardo tomorrow, the whole project itself, or the inescapable feeling that something very unpleasant waited for her on her return to New Orleans? She walked along the pier watching couples hand-in-hand, then hailed a taxi back to her hotel, hoping to get at least a little more sleep to clear her head.

Sunday morning, which felt like midnight Saturday on Maggie's jet-lagging body clock, started with mist and the threat of rain. She took a small boat over to Venice around eight o'clock. It was loaded with merchandise. Everything used or consumed on the islands still had to be ferried from the mainland or carried across the causeway.

As the boat approached the islands, Maggie saw the clock tower rising high in San Marcos Square. She wondered if Lucas had already started for the day and if he had begun to create his site maps. As they neared the docks, the oarsmen on the gondolas were sleepily preparing for the onslaught of tourists who would be arriving shortly for the guided tours through the streets of water and crumbling buildings. Some of the gondolas were painted black. According to folklore, beneath the black paint were the bright colors of a once powerful nation that was in perpetual mourning for its lost independence.

Maggie jumped from the motorboat, allowing herself the brief luxury of stepping back in time. She imagined merchants from all over Europe and Asia excitedly hawking their wares, vendors selling fruit and vegetables in the open-air market, senators racing to be on time for their meetings. Lost in the past, she bumped into a cart full of bottled water, candy, and postcards. The young man smiled, revealing a couple of missing front teeth.

"I'm sorry," Maggie mumbled.

"Ah, *Signorina*, postcards? Whole package, two dollars American," he said, unfolding a string of pictorial renditions of Venice.

"Oh, no, not today, but maybe another day soon," Maggie replied. He looked at her with only a hint of curiosity, noting the suitcase she dragged behind. He then turned to greet the tour group pouring from the boat that had just pulled up to the dock.

Maggie headed toward the campanile at the far end of the square. It was surrounded by wooden beams and sheets of bright blue plastic. In the basement of the tower could be the beginnings of an international career in bioarchaeology for her. At the very least, she might help find the solution to the mystery of who these people were and why they were hidden away for what might have been hundreds of years. Only a small part of Maggie's brain would acknowledge that she would also get a chance to spend a little time with Eduardo again.

A tall guard stood at the opening, blocking all entry. "Good morning," she said.

"*Bongiorno, Signorina.*"

"Are they working inside?"

"Yes, but no one can enter."

"Lucas Evans, is he here?"

"Ah, *Signor* Lucas, but of course."

"Can you get him?"

"One moment, please."

He stepped inside and returned a couple of minutes later with Lucas in tow. "Maggie, this is wonderful!" he greeted her. "I'm so glad you're here. It's incredible. Let me take your suitcase. I'll have someone carry it to the hotel. Come inside."

The entryway to the tower was a timber-lined vestibule that gave workers access to the small winding staircase leading to the top of the tower. As Maggie passed through the portal, she saw portions of a wall that had been removed, revealing a narrow passageway with steps leading downward. She heard a voice from below. It sounded familiar. She turned toward Lucas, but he had already disappeared around a sharp bend in the staircase. The stairs were dark and slippery. Something like mold or moss covered the wall where she steadied herself with her hand. She shuddered. For just a moment she felt claustrophobic.

Maggie probed her way down the dark staircase and around the bend. Looking up as she entered the small chamber, she stared straight into the eyes of Maura Stone, New Orleans' amateur archaeologist extraordinaire. A cold spot spread across the back of Maggie's neck. Intuition? The gift of fear? Why was she so uncomfortable all of a sudden? She only knew that she felt something unpleasant and disconcerting about seeing Maura. This feeling clearly was not something she had anticipated having in Venice on this project.

Maura looked at Maggie with the eyes of a wild rabbit, trapped in the beam of a car's headlights, wanting to flee but with no place to go.

Maggie didn't allow herself the luxury of glancing at the human remains spread around the room but turned abruptly, heading back up the steps to the light, Lucas at her heels.

"Damn you, Lucas," she sputtered as she reached the entrance. The guard stepped away a few yards, placing a discreet distance between himself and what he could tell was one angry female. "Just what in the hell is Maura doing here?"

"Now hold on, Maggie. She just got here yesterday. She's helping me with the mapping. You know I needed someone to do that."

"Yeah, but Maura? You never even hinted that you might bring her. In fact, I'm not sure I knew that you knew her. You have two minutes to explain this and it had better be good."

"Well," he began, "I met Maura a while back at some party. She's so interested in what we do. She soaks it up like a sponge. I feel good when I'm with her, better than I've felt in a while."

"Are you sleeping with her?"

"That's really none of your business," Lucas said in a tone Maggie had never heard from him before. Then he crossed the line. "Have I ever asked you if you still sleep with Dan?"

Maggie felt an instant burst of rage. Only rarely could something bring her to such a level of anger that quickly. When Lucas saw the fire in her eyes, he quickly pled, "Maggie I'm sorry. Slap me, punch me, anything. Just don't look like that. You're scaring me. If you want me to, I'll send her home today. Just say it."

Maggie stepped back a few feet, seething, and Lucas hung his head. His remorseful look gave her a sick feeling. She remembered Amy, his wife, and her death from the French Quarter car accident. "Look," she relented, "if this were a long-term project, I would demand that she go. She has no experience."

"Maggie," he interrupted, "she learns fast."

"Shut up and listen, Lucas. We are only going to be here about two more days. Keep her close to you and away from me. I can't put my finger on it, but there's something there that makes me uncomfortable. Haven't you noticed it? You used to be really good at picking up on those kinds of things. Whatever it is, I don't want to face it thousands of miles from home. I'm just not up to it right now. And one more thing, Lucas, Dan and I don't share a bed or breakfast anymore. That ended a long time ago."

"Maggie, I'm forever sorry I said that."

"Let's just go inside," she replied. As they entered the tower, she patted him twice on the shoulder. The second pat almost drove him through the brick wall. Working those arm weights was paying off.

Maura was squatting over in a corner of the chamber as they stepped inside. Maggie swallowed her aggravation and tried to be civil. "Hello, Maura. I'm surprised to see you." She turned abruptly toward Lucas before Maura could reply and spoke a little more softly. "O.K., hot shot, tell me all about it." It was then she began to look around the room and the aggravation she'd felt a few moments before started to dissolve.

Skeletons lay sprawled across the floor, filling the small room. Eduardo had been right. There were at least ten. Amazingly, some bodies still had a little desiccated tissue left on them. The bones were dark brown. Small bits of fabric clung to them. Maggie took a deep breath. The air smelled musty, even with two fans in the corner running full blast. The smell may have come from the dry adipocere she saw on the skeletons, the grayish-white, soapy substance sometimes formed after death from the separation of fatty adipose tissue. More often than not it could set up in a moist environment. Maggie's eyes traveled over the skeletons, evaluating them as she went. Eduardo's photographs had not done them justice.

She then looked up and down the walls. Watermarks confirmed seepage into the room. About four feet up on the easternmost wall, writing of some kind was etched into the stone. She took a closer look. The writing appeared to be a phrase, written twice, maybe in Latin, the letters about two inches tall. She turned toward Lucas. He shrugged his shoulders. "What does that mean, Lucas?"

"Not sure. Maybe a name. I'm working on that. One thing, though, Maggie, I think there's something you should know. I believe all of the skeletons are female."

"What?" Two worlds collided in Maggie's head. Her thoughts flashed back to the canals of New Orleans. It was like déjà vu. It took a moment to bring her mind back to Venice and the job at hand. Finally, she walked over to a short stool and sat down, trying to concentrate on what Lucas said and the scene before her. Her mind bounced back and forth from New Orleans to Venice, and everywhere it went were women's bodies and water.

Lucas quietly handed her his plan view of the remains, but Maggie already had a general map of the room and its contents in her head. The arrangement of the bodies was important, she reasoned, ignoring the inquisitive gaze from Lucas. "Treat this like a forensic case," she told herself. She stood up and began to pace back and forth in the cramped space as she tried to settle her mind. After a couple of minutes, she calmed down and began to consider the possibilities.

Most likely, she could expect one of two explanations for the spatial arrangement of the bodies in the chamber if the women had been placed there after they were already dead. They might have been lined up in rows on the floor. Perhaps some slight shifting of the bones could have occurred when water entered the room. Over time, once the tissue decayed, the lightweight, porous bones may have floated about. They probably would not have lost their general configuration, but bones in old coffin burials sometimes exhibited the most bizarre arrangement. Thigh bones could rotate, the backs of the bones facing upward. Tibiae could be found around the neck area. Skulls, because of their buoyancy, occasionally were found near the feet as a result of water movement in a coffin. But the skeletons in the clock tower's basement chamber were not in rows and certainly not in coffins.

The other possibility was that the Venetian women simply could have been dumped in a pile in the room. That clearly was not the case. Instead, the bodies, or what was left of them, were distributed randomly throughout the room.

Maggie continued looking. Two sets of remains over in a corner caught her attention. She moved toward the skeletons, bent down to look at them, and moaned softly. Not two, but three skeletons lay in the corner. A set of small, doll-like bones rested in the pelvic region of one of the women. They represented what was left of an almost full-term fetus, the fragile cranial bones collapsing into a small pile once the tissue decayed. She drew back for a moment, stunned by what she saw. She felt Maura's watchful eyes on her, refusing to turn toward Maura and reveal a vulnerability she seldom exposed. "What in the hell happened here?" she wondered.

Lucas's voice broke the quiet. "Maggie, we're almost ready to box the remains for transport to New Orleans." Thank goodness Eduardo had agreed, reluctantly, to allow her to analyze the remains in New Orleans. It would take considerable time to unravel this mystery and properly analyze the bones. She glanced Lucas' way but did not respond to his statement about shipping the bones. That was the least of her worries. She continued around the room, counting as she went.

Three in the corner. Two near the door. Four in the center of the room. One by the wall beneath the etching. The last one lying on her back against the western wall. At least eleven victims, maybe more if additional fetal remains were found with some of the others. They were young. A few were very young, each hip bone still in three pieces, not fused into one as it would be by the middle teenage years.

To herself she echoed, "What happened here?" Maggie felt a little nauseated, partly because of the musty air. She could understand why Dr. Lista, the Italian bioarchaeologist, got ill in this place. She wanted out and wanted out now. She headed toward the stairs, but Lucas called after her.

"Maggie."

Maggie turned, her look silencing him. Maura had yet to say a word. Maggie moved toward the doorway and up the dark staircase. She stumbled on the slippery surface, hitting her right knee hard on the stone steps. The realization that a hematoma was forming around her kneecap reminded her of why she had come there in the first place. She was trained to be objective. Eduardo had asked for her help. But she didn't have to like what she saw. No one could tell her how to feel. She continued up the stairs, groping her way toward the light and the fresh air.

Maggie stood at the front of the campanile for a moment, then began walking toward the two giant columns in the square and the dock beyond. She turned briefly and saw Lucas and Maura emerging from the small doorway of the tower. Lucas bumped his head on the timber when he ducked too late. He was clearly at least a foot taller than those who last entered the basement room as many as five hundred years before. The two of them walked in the direction of the church adjacent to the Doge's Palace. Maggie continued walking toward the dock, coming to a halt at the water's edge. She stared into its murky depths, trying to settle her mind. Who in the world were these women? What possible circumstances could have placed them in a room that had been sealed as long as five hundred years? Why weren't there any men there? Why had an ordinary room become their tomb? Had they drowned? She recalled that flooding was a constant problem in Venice. Had a flash flood trapped them inside? She was getting a stiff neck and a headache. She stared deeper into the waters and tried to clear her mind. It didn't work.

Maggie pondered, "Eduardo will be here soon. He probably expects me today. He knows that I always get up early. Maybe he has news that will help to solve this mystery. Whatever it is, I probably am not going to like what he has to say. Nothing can justify the presence of those young women in that place. Why couldn't it have been a bunch of soldiers with broken sword blades scattered about, the instruments of their honorable deaths? Is this why someone had to come half way around the world to investigate these bones, the remains of mere women, victims of a softer kill, not important enough to merit the interest of big-time archaeologists? Poor Eduardo, he might not be as happy to see me as he thought." Suddenly, the faces of the New Orleans victims swam before Maggie's eyes. "Two sets of victims with absolutely nothing in common except the fact that they were all women. Would it always be this way?"

Maggie had been standing at the dock for at least thirty minutes when the sound of a large motorized boat caused her to glance out toward the bay. Then she saw him. He was on the bow of the boat. You couldn't miss him. He would have stood out in any crowd. She had almost forgotten how beautiful he was. Time had been good to Eduardo. As the boat touched the dock, he jumped off and hurried toward her.

"Maggie, Maggie," he laughingly said. Engulfing her in a bear hug, he briefly kissed her on the lips, his full lower lip lingering just long enough to rouse old feelings deep inside of her. He grabbed her right hand with his left and smiled the smile that could have been delivered straight from Mount Olympus. Swinging her arm, he said, "It's great to see you, Maggie. When did you get here? I thought you might be here tomorrow. You haven't changed a bit. You look wonderful."

His English had improved considerably, his charm had diminished not a twit. "Liar, liar," she wanted to reply. Instead she answered, "Just a little while ago." She felt the cold heat of his wedding ring against her fingers and dropped his hand, pushing back the feelings that were rising. She spoke more sharply than she had planned. "Eduardo, I just came from the tower. Have you seen the skeletons in there?"

"Only briefly," he said, stiffening in reaction to her tone. "What's wrong?"

"They're all women."

"And?"

"Did you know that when you called me?"

"Maggie, I know you well enough not to second guess you. Just get it out. What is it?"

"Why couldn't someone here have examined these remains? There aren't that many of them. Surely they could have left their excavation project at Herculaneum long enough to do that."

"Now, wait a minute, Margaret Rose. Your cheeks are flaming. I see you've not lost that Irish temper. You are so Italian. Slow down."

"Don't you mock me, Eduardo. I'm dealing with a bunch of dead women in New Orleans right now, and it just strikes me as bizarre that these bodies are also all women."

"Maggie, it's not a conspiracy. There really was no one else to call at the moment. Honestly, they are all working at Herculaneum and Pompeii. I admit I thought that it would be great to see you again, but it's your expertise that's required here. This is important. Do you have any idea how I had to fight the committee to arrange for you to take these bones to the States? Of course you don't, but I felt like we were pulling apart the Iceman again. You know, the 5,000-year-old mummified mountain man they found in the Alps at the edge of the glacier?" Maggie didn't want to hear about a 5,000-year-old man whose story had flooded the news several years earlier. At the moment, he could have been Attila the Hun and she couldn't have cared less. She had a strong feeling that men were the culprits here and in New Orleans. She looked at Eduardo's face and knew he was telling her the truth, but she was still aggravated. She didn't want to think about the women for a while.

Hesitating briefly, she plunged forward. "Eduardo, let's take a walk."

"Sure, Maggie," he replied hesitantly.

The two of them headed away from the square, walking along the street toward the narrow bridge over the first canal. Stopping on the bridge, Eduardo said, "You know, this is the famous Bridge of Sighs."

"Seems as though I remember this from my first trip here," Maggie replied.

"Oh, that's right. You came soon after Antonio was born. God, he's beautiful, Maggie."

"I'm sure he is, Eduardo, and your wife, whose

name I don't even know—how is she?"

"Georgina is fine," he answered softly and went silent for only a moment. Then he changed the subject. Staring at the raised passageway between the Doge's Palace and the adjoining prison, he spoke quickly, "Your poet said that people could hear the prisoners moan as they passed over the canal toward the prison. We Italians do not believe that is true."

"My poet?" Maggie responded. "I believe Lord Byron was English, not American. Anyway, wouldn't it be great if such poetry had been written about the young women in the tower? I guess someone had something else in mind for them in the bowels of the earth. What do you think happened here, Eduardo?"

"I don't know, Maggie."

"What about the writing on the wall?"

"We believe it could be helpful in figuring out who these women are."

"Is it a name?"

"We don't think so. It's a phrase, perhaps a nickname. It's unusual. We are scanning some old documents to see if the words appear in any of them. We're trying to find the significance, if any, of the words' association with the bodies in the chamber. I'll let you know as soon as we know."

"Thanks. Could we head back now, Eduardo?"

Eduardo paused, cocked his head slightly and looked at her. "Sure, Maggie, anything you say."

It wasn't the bodies in the chamber or even those in New Orleans' canals that Maggie was thinking of at that moment. It was two other bodies, living ones, from long ago, but not so long as to forget the soft, full, coaxing lips, the heat of familiar hands, the leanness of young thighs pressed tightly together, the sweet sweat of youth. For just a moment, she almost lost control of her feelings. Instead, she laughed out loud. It had been too long since she had been with a man.

"Maggie, you amaze me. You still have that un-canny way of going from mad to glad in an instant. I miss that."

It was on the tip of Maggie's tongue to make a flip-pant remark, but instead she simply smiled and strolled ahead of him, almost skipping. She felt foolishly young for the first time in quite a while.

Maggie headed toward the tower with Eduardo trailing behind. Lucas and Maura walked out the church door, their heads bent closely to one another. They saw Maggie and moved toward her. She smiled broadly at both of them. They looked confused. Maggie especially noticed Maura's eyes on Eduardo as he came up behind her. She didn't like the knowing way Maura looked first at Eduardo and then back at her.

Though Maggie really wanted to speak to Eduardo longer, and, quite frankly, look at him a lot longer, she also knew that she was postponing the inevitable work on the recovery of the skeletal remains. Perhaps they could talk or meet again before she had to leave Venice. Eduardo stood around for a few minutes of polite con-versation, then explained that he had an urgent meeting on the mainland that required his presence. He left with a brief peck on the cheek for Maggie and a handshake for her which he held too long.

After a few hours of recording descriptions of each set of remains and looking over Lucas's drawings of the skel-etons, Maggie closed down the project for the day. She wearily followed Lucas and Maura back to the hotel, where the two of them were sharing a room. She was glad hers was on the second floor and theirs was on the first.

Chapter 8

It was raining lightly the next morning when Maggie woke. She raised her window and looked out onto the Grand Canal. Much larger than the other canals in Venice, it stretched across the city and out toward the Adriatic Sea. War ships must have come that way at one time, returning home. Some young woman may have stood right there where Maggie stood, looking from the same window, waiting for her soldier to appear.

Maggie thought about the women in the chamber. Though forensic speculation had always been a strength of hers, she could not come up with a reasonable explanation for the women's presence in the tower's basement chamber. Could they have been hiding from someone? Were they imprisoned there for some ghastly deed? The possibilities that came to mind were the same ones she had thought of yesterday, nothing new. She remembered the fetus, and her eyes unexpectedly filled with tears. She wiped them away roughly with her shirttail. She had chosen this life she led. She had dead women on two continents, and she was getting weepy over a death that had occurred hundreds of years ago. Now she was thinking about babies instead of just dreaming about them. "Straighten up, Maggie," she said to herself. "Get on with the show." She closed the window harder than she meant to, took a deep breath, and walked out the door, shutting it gently behind her.

Maggie slipped quietly down the hallway and the stairs. The small dining room adjacent to the hotel's entryway was open. She poured a cup of weak coffee. No one was around to suggest breakfast but the rolls on the nearby table more than likely were free for the taking. She took one. Today was the day they were going to start boxing the bones, and no one was going to pick up any bone without her approval. She opened the hotel door and stepped out into the day.

Only a few people were walking along the narrow streets. In the piazza, the Doge's Palace was deserted. The oars on the gondolas at the dock rested unattended, the waters in the canals quiet. As she approached the Bridge of Sighs, Maggie saw Maura standing quietly, looking into the dark waters of the canal. She walked up to Maura and spoke. "Good morning, Maura." Maura slowly turned and gazed at Maggie. She had a strange, far-away look on her face. Maggie spoke again. "Do you like the canals?"

"Of course," Maura replied softly. "I find the waters soothing, cleansing."

"Interesting adjectives for such a dirty, dark abyss," Maggie thought. "Where is Lucas?" she asked.

"Still in bed, I guess." Maura replied.

"Well, it's time to start on the skeletons."

"Do you want me to go get him?" Maura asked.

"No. He had a rough day yesterday. Let him sleep. Come on. I'll show you what to do." The two women headed toward the tower, not speaking, their body language signaling a temporary truce.

Maggie and Maura approached the campanile. The tower guard was already in place, probably having slept there all night. He made no movement to stop either of the two women, obviously aware that Maggie was a woman to be reckoned with and not willing to go through any unpleasantries so early in the morning. He gave the two of them a brief nod as they entered the tower.

Once more Maggie made her way down the winding, shadowy staircase, stepping aside at the foot of the stairs to let Maura enter the chamber first. She saw the shipping boxes in a corner of the chamber and figured that Lucas and Maura must have put them together late yesterday evening. Maura stopped beside her in the doorway at the foot of the steps. Maggie turned toward her and said, "Let's start with the skeleton closest to the door and work our way toward the back. That way, we'll clear a path as we go. First, we need to label each box with the same number that Lucas assigned to that skeleton so we won't get confused about which one was where later on. The skeleton in this corner is number five. Let's get started."

"Maggie, are you sure you don't want me to wake Lucas?"

"Maura, what did I just say?"

"You said let's get started."

"That's right. Now, skeleton number five is fragile. No tendons or ligaments are preserved. So the bones are all separated from each other. Some of the teeth are missing. The sockets for those teeth are very sharp around the edges. That tells me the teeth fell out after death. Once we pack the skull, we'll look for loose teeth beneath the body. Now, help me with this bag."

Maura picked up the bag. For the first time, Maggie noticed Maura's hands. The nails were short and perfectly manicured. Maura interrupted her thoughts.

"What are you using the bag for?" Maura asked her.

"I'm placing the bag around the skull in order to prevent the loss of any more teeth or other evidence associated with the head region."

"Evidence?"

"Evidence, information, call it whatever you like. I'm treating these women like forensic cases. That's probably what they are, five-hundred-year-old forensic cases. Put on these gloves and slide this bag beneath the skull when I raise it a little."

They worked in silence for an hour or more, carefully placing bones in bags and marking the bags as they went along, right hand, left hand, right foot, left foot. They had almost finished packaging the first skeleton when Lucas appeared in the doorway.

"Glad to see things are proceeding well down here," he said sheepishly. They both looked up at him and then lowered their heads without speaking.

By noon they had managed to box three sets of remains, taking additional notes as they went. They would be finished with two more by dark and could take out the other five or so in one more day if they worked steadily. Maggie could head home the day after tomorrow as planned.

The skeletons had been fairly easy to package. All small, all with only a little clothing here and there. One with a cross, another with a broach. One with a ring on her toe. Whoever had done this to them had at least not robbed them.

Everyone was unusually quiet that day, hardly talking as the day wore on. It was hard to figure out the relationship between Maura and Lucas, Maggie thought, and she didn't really have the energy to address it. That could wait for New Orleans.

Eduardo made a brief appearance that afternoon but hurried away, mumbling something about a meeting he had to attend. Maggie was disappointed but had to finish the job she came to do.

They finished packing the fifth skeleton around 3:30 p.m., having stopped only once for a brief lunch purchased from a stall in the piazza. Maggie called it quits for the day.

Lucas seemed anxious to make amends for their disagreement the day before and said, "Maggie, Maura and I are scouting out some of the cemeteries around here. Are you interested in going with us?" Though Maggie loved the carvings on old gravestones and had collected various rubbings from cemeteries across the world, she was not anxious to spend her little free time in Venice with Lucas and Maura. She was still a little irritated with Lucas for bringing Maura. She had hoped to spend some time of her own with her old friend now that he seemed to be regaining some interest in things other than drinking and tattoos.

"Thanks," she said, "but I'm heading to the glassworks. I want to catch the blowers before they close for the day." Venice was known for its beautiful glassware, especially the decanter sets and wine glasses in rich reds, blues, and greens that were highly collectable during the Victorian era. Maggie loved them. Lucas looked at her as though waiting for her to ask the two of them along, but she didn't. Ever since Maggie had read *The Glass Menagerie* she had been fascinated by the forms that hot glass could take and had only been able to spend a few minutes watching the process on her first trip to Venice. She wanted to go alone.

Maggie left the tower, bought a bottle of water from a street vendor and walked toward the glass factory, enjoying the sounds of Italian words punctuated with the Venetian dialect.

Entering through the factory's showroom, she spoke to a sales clerk about the possibility of visiting the factory. The clerk ushered Maggie toward the back of the building and pointed toward the small enclosed area beyond a side door. There, a group of tourists were waiting to be led into the factory. Maggie blended into their group. Blended, that is, as well as she might with the cohort of tall, blond, blue-eyed Scandinavians.

They entered a small, hot room where a young man, apparently an apprentice, judging by his age, was gently blowing through a long tube to which he had attached some molten glass. As Maggie watched him, the glass at the end of the tube grew in size and took the shape of a pale pink vase about four inches tall. The glass-blower then snapped the end of the vase with a cutter and placed it alongside several others, which would later be polished and hand decorated.

She watched the young man while he worked on two more pieces. The art of glass blowing had been passed down from one generation to the next for hundreds of years, and sons of sons followed in their fathers' footsteps.

Reluctantly, Maggie exited the hot factory into the showroom and looked for a vase similar to the ones the apprentice had created. In a corner display case, she found one with gold trim around the top lip and a delicate pink and white flower with raised petals on the front. It was just the right size and easily would fit into her small suitcase for the trip home. The hard part would be finding a place for it where Tango could not go.

She headed out into the night alone, wishing for someone with whom she could walk along the streets, wondering why Eduardo had not stayed longer that day or at least suggested dinner for the two of them. Maggie caught a whiff of the familiar fish smells that reminded her so much of New Orleans. The small restaurant she had passed just down the street a little earlier surely would have wine and the fish of the day.

Chapter 9

Eduardo did not return to the tower. Maggie thought his behavior a little odd, but who was she to judge what devils he might be keeping at bay? She spoke with him by phone on her third and last day in Italy. "It will be difficult, Eduardo," she said, "but I promise to return with the skeletons in two weeks."

"I know you'll be back, Maggie. Maybe then we can have a private conversation and talk about old times." In his voice, Maggie thought she heard a hint of sadness, maybe even regret, but she had probably misunderstood as usual. He lingered with the conversation, not really saying anything of substance, almost as though he hated to hang up the phone. She was glad at that point that he was not at the piazza in person. She might have swooned right there in the middle of the square.

The final day of packing the skeletons had been a long one and, briefly, Maggie regretted taking the time to visit the glass factory the day before. They finished around 6

p.m. and then readied the boxes for transport to Marco
Polo Airport. At least they had finished collecting the
remains. Maybe things would go smoothly when they
got back home. If she was lucky, Rodney Durham and
his camera equipment would have been run over by a
streetcar—the equipment crushed, but Rodney just
slightly incapacitated for several months. Enough time
to give her a breather from his incessant sudden appear-
ances. Enough time to slough off the uncomfortable
feeling she had about him.

Around 7 p.m. Maggie and Lucas loaded the shipping boxes onto the boat they had rented and headed toward the mainland. Their flight didn't leave until
noon the next day, but they needed to get the boxes
to the cargo area at the airport that evening and make
sure the permits Eduardo had secured for them were
all in order. Since the papers were in Italian, Maggie
figured they would pass through with no problem. For
once, she was right. No one challenged anything as the
agents stamped the sealed boxes and loaded them onto
carts that disappeared into the cargo bay. Maggie made
a mental note to check with the airline in Atlanta to
make certain all of the boxes made it to the States.

On the way back to Venice, the hum of the boat
seemed somewhat soothing as Maggie stood on its
bow. She thought about the significance of the project and the Venetian women. The irony of taking them
to the United States was not lost on her. They would
be world travelers and wouldn't even know it. If they
lived in Venice five hundred years ago, and the preliminary evidence seemed to point to that, most people still
thought the world was flat at that time. Did removing
them from their island chamber serve any higher good?
Sometimes Maggie doubted the importance of scientific
researchers' insatiable need to study anything ancient.

Were the women better off just being left alone? She was not so naive as to believe that hundreds of anthropologists would not have jumped at the chance to study the women from the tower. Since they were to be removed anyway, no matter who did it, the chance to try to help solve the mystery of their deaths was one of the main things that drew Maggie to the project—that and, she had to admit, the chance to see Eduardo one more time. But, in addition to solving the mystery of their deaths, to examine the women's remains for pathologies might actually add some small knowledge to the history of disease. The scientist in Maggie felt lucky for the opportunity to do ground-breaking work and the woman in her felt guilty for scrutinizing the women so closely. When she got back to her hotel around 11 p.m., she fell into bed without a bath.

Maggie experienced guarded relief as the plane lifted from the runway at Marco Polo Airport. She was headed back to New Orleans with enough human remains to entirely block the entrance to her lab. Her rash promise to Eduardo about the turnaround time now seemed ridiculously brief. She decided to look on the bright side. Maybe things back home had gone smoothly and Dan had helped to catch a killer, though she knew he would have called her if he had.

The flight back to New Orleans was uneventful. Maggie decided at Gatwick to do something she hadn't intended to do. She upgraded her ticket to business elite. She left Lucas and Maura in economy. She was certain they didn't want to see her anyway. She figured that the upgrade would leave her just about breaking even on the project. No one ever said there was a lot of money in her field.

The recliner in her section was soft blue leather.

She collapsed into it. She got the attendant's attention and ordered two bottles of water. She wanted plenty of liquid in her veins before she began a serious discussion with Mr. Merlot.

Maggie, Lucas, and Maura arrived in Atlanta in the late evening of the day they left Venice. Maggie was still not used to the time change and hoped her jet lag would not be too severe. The one-hour flight to New Orleans was quiet except for a few bumps and shifts of the plane as it navigated around a tropical storm brewing in the Gulf.

Maggie had checked in Atlanta to make sure their ten boxes had made it aboard their flight home. The boxes were on the plane before the passengers were, as the control tower watched the weather patterns in the Gulf. The storm had stalled off the coast of Florida, and no one knew whether it would head up the east coast from there or make life hell in the Gulf. Just what New Orleans needed, more water in the canals. Maggie was growing very weary of water.

The plane landed in New Orleans. Lucas had left his SUV at the airport, and it was perfect for transporting the bones to the lab. He went to retrieve it from long-term parking while Maggie and Maura stood in awkward silence at the cargo loading door waiting for his return. Maura shifted her gaze back and forth from Maggie to the driveway where Lucas would appear. Maggie just didn't feel like conversation and pretended to be studying the shipping manifest detailing their unusual cargo. Relieved, she spotted Lucas's SUV just as Maura appeared on the verge of speaking. The fire-engine red SUV stood out among the more typical white, black, and beige ones queuing up to the curb.

They quickly loaded the boxes into Lucas' SUV and Lucas and Maura dropped Maggie off at airport parking. Her Karmann Ghia looked a little out of place among the newer vehicles in the lot, but she took great comfort in seeing it, an old friend. She had only a few hours before time to head to the lab and start on the analysis of the Venetian women. She also had to catch up on whatever had been going on in the coroner's office and provide final reports on the New Orleans canal cases. There simply wasn't enough time in her days to do all of this. Handling cases from the coroner's office and continuing her bioarchaeology business might need a re-evaluation in the near future. Maybe she wasn't super woman after all. Maybe one of them had to go. Which would it be?

Brutus and Tango were delirious when Maggie pulled into her building and got out of the car. Brutus lunged for her, slobbering all over her travel clothes. Tango hung back but seemed on the verge of actually lying down to be petted. He soon got over that. Maggie lugged her suitcase upstairs and saw the note from Moses on the kitchen counter. "Welcome home. No problems. Brutus and Tango have been fed. Moses."

Maggie headed for a long, slow bath. It might be a while before she could have that kind of luxury again. The soft light from the candles she had placed on a stool near the tub and the wonderful glass of merlot reinforced why she was glad to be alive. Home was great. Life was good.

Musty odors of the ancient dead mingled with the bleach of recently sanitized instruments in Maggie's lab. She and Lucas had almost completed their analysis of the Venetian women's fragile bones, now stacked on carts throughout the room. Day after day they had measured the bones, calculated height, estimated age, and pored over the skeletons for pathologies.

On the fifth day of analysis, Lucas picked up the skull of a young woman, probably between the ages of 15 and 17. "Maggie, what are these little indentations on her forehead?"

"Those are skeletal lesions that suggest she may have had venereal syphilis." Lucas quickly put down the skull.

"You're kidding, right?"

"Not at all. You see, syphilis can hide in the body after making a brief appearance as a genital canker through infection during sexual intercourse. It might not present any major physical manifestation for years but eventually can affect the skeletal system. Look at her femora and tibiae. Then check out her clavicles. Lucas gingerly picked up the leg bones and noted their swollen appearance. On the backs of the collar bones, he saw deep furrows.

"O.K. I give up. I can understand the long bones, but what are these sunken areas on the backs of her clavicles?"

"Those are sites of bone loss where syphilitic cysts may have been anchored. I saw clavicles like this one time on a forensic case, a thirteen-year-old kid. He was a known prostitute who died a violent death. His killer was never found. But here's the real clue." Maggie picked up the x-ray of the fetus that had been found with the young woman. "You see those tooth buds, there?" Lucas nodded yes. "Look at the biting edge of the upper central incisors. Can you see them? They are really small."

"Yes, I see them. What about them?"

"Do you see how they are curved, almost cup-like on the edge?"

"Sort of."

"Children born with congenital syphilis have teeth that are shaped like that. Now, I can't say for certain that this child's teeth are definitely those of a child with congenital syphilis, but if you put together that information with what is going on with the mother, it might be true."

"Maggie, are you saying the mother can pass it on to the child?

"Yes."

"Have you ever seen anything like this before?

"No, but, fortunately, I have never had to work on a mother and her child before either.

"I didn't know that syphilis was even found in Europe at the time these women lived," Lucas responded.

"The debate is still out on that. Some say it came to the Old World when Columbus returned from his maiden voyage to the New World. Others say it was in the Old World before then. All I know is what the skeleton is telling me. Do you want to see something else?"

"I don't know....do I?" Lucas answered reluctantly.

"Look at this female, burial nine. She's even more unusual than the first case."

"Am I ready for this, Maggie?" Lucas said.

"It's according to how much you like bone pathology."

"I don't know if I like it at all, but since you are all wound up, go ahead and show me."

Maggie walked over to another tray. Few people other than physical anthropologists and some bioarchaeologists were interested in the information ancient skeletons could reveal about diseases.

"Look at these foot bones, the metatarsals. Tell me what you see."

"Foot bones."

"Funny. What else?"

"Well, they look a little skinny."

"Good eye. They are a 'little skinny.' We biological anthropologists call that 'wasting.' The only time I have ever seen that before is on a case of leprosy in a medieval skeletal collection in England."

"Don't they call that Hansen's Disease these days?"

"Yes, here in America they do," Maggie said, "but some researchers in Europe still refer to it as leprosy."

"What causes it?"

"*Mycobacterium leprae.*"

"Myco what?"

"It's a mycobacterium closely related to the one that results in tuberculosis. Leprosy certainly was around during the sixteenth century and, in fact, has been recorded for more than two thousand years. Biblical references to leprosy caused it to be confused with many other skin diseases in early history. The misdiagnosis was used to brand persons as 'unclean.' Only in the last few decades has the biblical curse been treated in a more compassionate manner. Bone samples might tell us if she actually had the disease. If this young woman had any skin lesions, they could have branded her as unclean." Lucas rolled his eyes. He loved the archaeology of a project but had little patience for Maggie's bone lecture.

"Maggie, I have a great idea. How about lunch?"

Maggie knew she had lost him at that point and said, "Sure. Let's go." As they walked down the street, she thought about the young women. Of course the pathologies were informative for research, but for forensic purposes, the kinds of diseases the women may have contracted didn't really matter so much as how they spent their daily lives. If they were criminals, they would have been imprisoned in some kind of jail, wouldn't they? Maybe they would have been stoned. Maybe they were gypsies who had infuriated the locals. What if they were prostitutes? What would have been the fate of a pregnant prostitute?

Maggie returned to the lab without Lucas. He was done for the day. She studied the few fabric remnants they had found. They would be analyzed by a textile expert across town. The results would probably provide only the type of weave and what natural fibers had been used to construct the garments. What mattered most was how the women died. Back again to the cause of death. What was it? No sign of trauma was present on any of the skeletons, not a single broken bone. Something didn't add up. Maggie felt she probably would have the same bad luck with the Venetian victims as she was having with the modern canal cases. No clear leads. But these women from two different worlds whose deaths were separated by as much as five hundred years continued to plague most of her waking and many of her sleeping hours.

For almost two weeks, Maggie's days were filled with the five-hundred-year-old corpses and four unsolved murder cases. The frustration and long days at the lab were making both Lucas and Maggie a little frayed around the edges. But she was already a little past her target date to get the bones back to Eduardo. She had to finish the analysis and fly back to Venice. At night, she fell into bed with barely a quick rub for Brutus and Tango. They were not happy either.

Chapter 10

The land phone was ringing and the cell phone was vibrating. The ringing got louder and louder as Maggie struggled from a deep sleep. Her cell phone danced off the edge of her bedside table, and someone was jamming her doorbell over and over again. Whoever was at the door was hollering now, and Brutus was going nuts. His Baskerville howl finally compelled Maggie to clear her head. She grabbed a robe, ignoring both phones, and hurried downstairs. She remembered to turn off the new alarm system before peering through the peephole. It was Lucas. She opened the door and saw at once that he was visibly distraught.

"Maggie, it's Maura. She's dead, in the canal. There's another body there, too. Come on. Let's go."

Maggie dressed quickly, her mind racing. Two more victims. She couldn't think straight. Her head began to pound.

When Maggie and Lucas arrived on the scene, at least a hundred people lined the banks on both sides. Jimmy O'Malley's head stuck out above the others and he looked their way. He moved toward them, but Maggie shook her head. Jimmy understood and turned away. Rodney Durham was running down the street with his cameraman, heading in the opposite direction from the canal.

Maggie thought about Maura. She had last seen her a week ago. She had been stopping by the lab for the last two weeks to help Lucas with the sorting and inventory of the Venice cases, but usually in the evenings after Maggie had already left. Maggie had stayed later than usual one day and they bumped into each other at the door to the morgue. They had exchanged brief hellos and goodbyes.

Why had the murderer killed Maura? Though attractive, she clearly was almost a generation removed from the other victims. And what about the second body? Two at one time? Nothing made sense. Maggie and Lucas didn't talk as they walked toward the edge of the canal. The pain in Lucas's face was evident.

A coroner's body bag lay at the edge of the canal and obviously contained one of the victims. Another bag lay nearby, but it was not a body bag. It looked like some kind of large canvas duffel bag and had probably been white or beige before it entered the filthy water in the canal.

Dan approached Maggie and Lucas as they neared the canal's edge, drawing them away from the investigators. He looked at Lucas and spoke quietly. "Lucas, are you sure you want to be here? This is not something you have to see."

"Look, Dan, I'm fine," Lucas said, his voice hardly above a whisper.

Maggie grabbed Lucas's hand. "What about the other victim?" she said.

"We don't know," Dan answered. "The duffel bag was caught on some debris near where Maura was found. The man who found her just dragged it ashore. He was shocked to see another body inside the duffel bag and pulled the drawstring tight again. We barely looked inside the bag when we got here. We'll inspect it more closely back in the morgue. Browning is waiting for us there to do the autopsies. Maggie, can you come to the autopsies?" Of course she would be there.

Dan turned toward Lucas. "Lucas, it's up to you whether you come or not."

"I know, Dan. But I'll be there. This has to stop. Someone has to catch the person who did this. If it gets too hard, I'll walk away." Dan nodded and turned back to the investigators.

Sidney, the lead coroner's investigator, once again supervised the removal of the bodies. The body bag with Maura in it was placed in one vehicle. The canvas bag was quickly transferred intact to another body bag and placed in the other coroner's van. Maggie and Lucas watched and then returned to Lucas's SUV for the short trip to the morgue. "Too many dead bodies lately," Maggie muttered to herself. They had to catch this monster. Not a single word passed between Lucas and Maggie on the short drive. She didn't know what to say anyway, considering her feelings about Maura.

The morgue seemed gloomier than usual and not a place Maggie wanted to be. Lucas quickly disappeared inside before she had a chance to tell him how sorry she was about Maura. She still didn't know the depth of their relationship.

Browning was already suited up and her assistant was transferring Maura's body from the x-ray room when Maggie entered the lab. Detectives milled around the corner of the room. "The x-rays that we just took show no evidence of a wound or a metal object, so we'll start the autopsy," Browning said.

In the light of the cold room, Maura's face was like any other face at autopsy, totally devoid of expression, all muscles loose and unresponsive. She reminded Maggie of the photos she had seen of Marilyn Monroe after she died, almost unrecognizable as the glamorous movie star. Though not a movie star, in life Maura surely must have had a following. In death, she had only Lucas, who stepped close to the table, took one brief look, then walked out the door.

Browning followed the same routine as in all of her autopsies. First, she gave the brief overview of the victim's appearance. In Maura's case, she noted, "Small, white female, straight black hair, no rigor, some lividity on the back near lumbar vertebrae. No outward signs of trauma." She noticed, as Maggie did, some foamy bubbles at the corner of Maura's mouth and commented briefly into the mike. After taking the trace evidence samples from across Maura's body, she opened the larynx and throat region, grabbing Maggie's attention because she was deviating from her normal protocol. She usually saved that region for later in the autopsy. In the throat, they saw fluid again. Working swiftly, Browning opened the chest cavity and moved straight to the lungs. Frothy edema was present there as well. She spoke into the mike, "Cause of death: drowning. Manner of death unknown."

Browning continued the autopsy following her normal routine, though it seemed halfheartedly. She even checked for the tattoos they had come to expect. Maura had no tattoos, but she did have a small scar on the tip of one of her fingers. Just for a moment, it looked like a tattoo. It was about the size of the end of a pencil eraser and easily could have been a burn scar. Nothing else marred her body. Browning glanced at Maggie as she removed Maura's shoes and saw her well-manicured toenails, which reminded Maggie of Maura's neatly trimmed fingernails she had noticed earlier.

Browning finished with Maura and rolled the cart containing her body to the next processing station. Fingerprints and other trace evidence samples would be collected there by the assistants who helped Browning in multiple death cases. Browning moved on to the other cart. She was tired, plagued again by her allergies. Her dogged determination kept her going.

The fact that Maura had drowned threw another wrench into Maggie's theory. Hell, she had no theory now. Couldn't figure out what was going on. She had never felt so helpless. She decided to step outside for a moment to talk to Lucas. Sidney eyed her as she walked toward the door. He looked as though he wanted to speak but hesitated. He seemed especially jittery.

Lucas was nowhere to be found. He must have gone home or gone somewhere to get drunk. Either way, he probably didn't want to see Maggie, she thought. He would remember what she had said about Maura, and they would both have to struggle to fill some awkward silences.

Maggie turned and headed back toward the autopsy room. Browning was in the middle of her preliminary observations. "I'll be damned, another blunt trauma to the head. Would someone give this sack of manure a gun so we can at least figure out what the hell he's using on these women?" Even Maggie was surprised by her outburst. Browning looked sideways at Maggie. "Don't worry, I just turned off the recorder to sound off for a minute. But what's going on in this city? Six victims in the canals and not a murderer in sight." She shook her head and went on. "I'm about to turn the recorder back on but before I do, gentlemen, please find this slimy little bastard soon, or we are going to run out of morgue space. Everyone clear on that?" The detectives nodded.

Browning finished the autopsy on the white female from the duffel bag and began to check for tattoos again. She found what she was searching for, a small circle with what looked like a spinning top or tornado in its center. It was half hidden between the index and middle fingers of the left hand. The professional manicure job on the nails seemed oddly out of place on the short, stubby fingers. Not as attractive as the other victims who had been identified already, she still had an innocence about her. She couldn't possibly have been a day over fifteen, as the x-rays of her hands showed incomplete growth of the ends of the metacarpals, the first row of tubular bones in the hands.

Maggie wanted to strangle the guy who did this. Strangle him and dump his body in the Gulf of Mexico. Better yet, leave him alive, tie him up, nick a spot or two to draw blood and *then* dump him in the Gulf. The sharks would take care of the rest. She left the morgue in a dark mood. It would be a while before she could smile again. She looked for Dan but didn't see him. Instead, she felt the presence of someone behind her in the shadows of the building. It was Sidney.

"You need a ride, Miss Maggie?"

"No, Sidney, I'm looking for Dan."

"He left twenty minutes ago."

"Oh, really." She turned abruptly and headed back to the lab. She saw Browning gathering her personal belongings. "Doc, could I get a ride home with you?" Maggie whispered.

"Sure, Maggie. We both smell about the same. You're not in that great car?"

"No, I came with Lucas and he left. I thought I could catch Dan, but he's gone, too. Sidney offered, but quite frankly, given a choice, I would rather ride an alligator home."

"Let's go," she replied.

They walked out together as Browning's assistants continued their work on the two bodies. Sidney was nowhere to be found. Maggie was glad. She didn't want to hurt his feelings, but she didn't need his attention on top of everything else. She was surprised that Rodney Durham was not there either and wondered where the scum and his cameraman had gone.

Browning dropped Maggie at her door and she let herself in. Moses was long gone and had already fed Brutus and Tango, according to the note he'd taped to the newel post at the bottom of the stairs. Even if he had not left a note, she easily could tell that Brutus had been fed. His sluggish gait as he made his way down the staircase was a giveaway. Maggie sat down at the bottom of the stairs and he tried fruitlessly to figure out a way to get into her lap. Though his nose told him where she had been, his instinct told him something was seriously wrong. He licked her face and her arms and her hands while she sat still and silent. She was too overwrought to think straight. Tango also sensed her mood. Maggie felt something rub against her shoulder and turned in time to watch him scoot two steps up, then stop and stare back at her with his streetwise eyes.

To get her mind off Maura, Maggie decided to clean house and look for Dorothy Brown's file. The missing file had her perplexed. Dorothy was the first victim found in the canals and was the only one with a cinderblock tied to her. The file had not been under Maggie's bed when she looked there after returning from Venice. She simply could not figure out what had happened to it. Maybe she had thrown it down somewhere after that disturbing interruption of sleep by the would-be intruder. Behind a chair, under the stairwell—who knew?

Three hours and two glasses of merlot later, Maggie had a cleaner house. Most of the dust had been routed from the corners. All the dishes were washed and put away, and the bathroom was all shiny. But there was no sign of Dorothy Brown's file. She sat down at the top of the stairs and tried to remember the last time she had seen the file. It was the day she left the lab with all four files. She had placed them on the front seat of her car and caught the bus to the Quarter. When she returned, she found her ragtop cut, though the files were still there. But, were all of them there? She wished she had counted them that day. What if the person who cut her top did so just to get Dorothy's file? Well, wouldn't that be great to suggest to Dan. "I can't handle this. I'm the bone detective, not the homicide detective," Maggie mumbled to herself. It was not like Maggie to misplace anything, much less an entire file. Something was not adding up.

The few details she had on the cases kept running through her head. Six victims, four tattoos, four blunt force, one drowning, one unknown. Five below the age of thirty. One above the age of forty. No clear evidence of sexual assault on any of them. Three of them still unidentified. Maggie threw up her hands and shouted, "Hell! I give up. I'm throwing out all of those profiler books. Nothing adds up. Nothing."

She decided to have a third glass of merlot. She was in her own home. She was not drinking and driving, and she didn't want to think about anything anymore tonight. She just wanted to sleep. The fact that she had eaten little or nothing all day might produce interesting results. It did, all right. Three or four sips from the glass and out she went, cold.

Chapter 11

A week had passed since Maura's body had floated up in the canal. The media were going crazy with the cases. Several reporters had left messages on Maggie's phone. Jimmy O'Malley knew better than to do so, and Rodney Durham was conspicuously absent. That week ended with no new victims in the canal, but the authorities were still no closer to solving the cases. Reality set in. In contrast to the high drama of prime-time television, where all cases were solved in less than 45 minutes if you discounted commercials, they might never solve the canal cases. Some serial killers go to their graves with their secrets. When Maggie opened her eyes that Friday morning, she could not believe it was already 8 a.m. She hadn't slept that late in years. It felt good after a restless week of worry, but she had so much to do even losing an hour could make a difference. She had to finish the final report on the young women from Venice and help get their bones packed for shipment back to Venice. She had not heard from Eduardo, but she knew he must be pacing up and down as more than two weeks had passed since she had begun the analysis. Maggie thought he would more than likely understand if he knew what had happened to Maura, but she did not contact him. She was supposed to accompany the bones back to Venice. So was Lucas, but he probably wouldn't go. Too painful for him. Maggie had seen him only once since Maura's death, and he had seemed preoccupied. They had hardly talked that day. She only hoped that he'd be able to work through the loss of Maura coming so soon after the death of his wife. Whether he would plunge back into the bottle again was anyone's guess.

Indeed Lucas would not return to Venice. Maggie couldn't get him to go, though she really didn't try very hard to convince him. He was busy, he said, arranging disposition of Maura's estate. She was confused by that until he told her that, surprisingly, Maura had left everything she owned to him in a will dated just prior to their trip to Venice. "Everything" included a nineteenth-century house in the heart of the Garden District. If it had been anyone but Lucas, Maggie would have been jealous, but not Lucas. It was about time something went his way. She prepared to leave for Venice without him.

The skeletal remains had been repacked and were ready for transport to the airport, but Maggie was a little apprehensive that something might have gotten misplaced since they had to turn around the analysis so fast. Lucas personally handled all the packing. He had assured her he did not need her help with the packing and that he had followed her guidelines explicitly. In fact, he had been working very late at the lab each night for the last week. Maggie was surprised that he wanted to be there after what had happened to Maura, but he insisted that packaging the Venetian bones was good for him. "Besides," he told her, "Maura is long gone. Dan gave permission for her to be released and I had her cremated. She said in her will that was what she wanted."

Maggie thought it strange that Dan had released her body, but he and Lucas clearly had discussed it. What she found odd was that a person such as Maura who was so conscious of her looks and involved in preservation of the past wanted to be reduced to a pile of ash. But it was her body. The one thing we ought to have the right to control, since we have no power over death, is the final disposition of our bodies. It almost cheats death, just a little. The grim reaper can take our last breath, but hands off the rest of me, please.

Maggie asked Dan to help her get the bones to the airport. "Sure," he said. "I'll be happy to carry the boxes. Do you want to ride with me, too? It would be like old times. I could turn on the siren and people would stop on a dime and clear the streets for us."

"What's gotten into you lately? How would that look to people when you're running for one last term as 'always fair even when the weather's foul Farrington'?"

"I guess you're right," he said. Maggie hadn't the heart to tell him that she'd seen a couple of his campaign signs defaced with the "fair" and "foul" transposed. She had stopped immediately and thrown them into the trunk of her car.

"I don't know, though," he continued. "This killing spree has worn me out and made me wonder if I'm even up to one more term. It might not matter if I am or not if something doesn't happen soon. The mayor is screaming for action and the public is scared. Hell, *I'm* even having nightmares. It's funny, though, the killer must be on a hiatus. No one has been found since Maura."

"Well, when I get back from Venice in a few days, maybe we can make progress on the canal victims without distractions."

"Is your friend Eduardo, going to be there?"

"Dan, that's the first time in years you've even mentioned his name. Yes, he'll be there, but for heaven's sake, he's married with a child. Besides, how is that any of your business?"

For just a moment, Maggie glimpsed something wild in his eyes and then it was gone. She scolded herself. "There you go again, Maggie, getting defensive. You're destined to grow old with only a dog and a cat."

"Let's get your car loaded," she said. "Then we can put a few boxes in mine. These all go in special cargo and I can take them to the airport today and not have to worry about them tomorrow when I leave." They packed Dan's car in silence, and he helped her put the last three boxes in the front seat of hers. They were all sealed just as Lucas had said they would be. Their bland appearance would not attract the curious and the permits for their travel had been completed already.

Dan led the way to the airport. At one point, he touched his siren for just a moment, stuck his left hand out the window and waved Maggie around. As she pulled up beside him, he pretended to be scolding her. He shouted, "Excuse me, ma'am, but do you have a permit to drive this vehicle outside a circus tent?" She could have killed him. She sped ahead of him on the expressway, leaving him to find her later at the airport.

As Maggie exited the expressway, heading toward the airport beyond, she caught a whiff of something dead. At first she thought she had imagined it, but she had spent too long around the dead to be wrong. Maybe it was just road kill, or something in the lab that had gotten on one of the boxes. She glanced at them but saw nothing obvious. The odor was there, and then it was gone. Maybe she *did* just imagine it.

Dan found his way to the cargo door at the airport, and she was waiting there for him with the airport agent. She didn't speak to him as they removed the boxes. The two of them placed the boxes on the loading cart and walked with the cargo agent as he moved them toward the counter. Maggie handed him the paperwork and explained to him how she would be on the same plane as the boxes that would be leaving the next day for Atlanta and then would be transferred to a 767 for the trip to Gatwick. At Gatwick, other permits were required to transport the remains to Venice. Eduardo had already taken care of those. They would be waiting for her across the ocean.

When Eduardo met Maggie in Venice, he was as charming as usual but in a bit of a hurry. The workmen were waiting for them at the tower to seal the young women's remains in the basement chamber.

"Eduardo, why the hurry with this?"

"You won't like this, Maggie, but this is the way it's going to be. The young women will be reinterred in the chamber at the bottom of the tower."

"I thought you said they might receive an honorable burial in one of the church cemeteries away from the square."

"That was suggested at one time, but the decision has been made to return them to the tower and have a monument placed out front."

"The decision has been made by whom?"

"Maggie, you are an anthropologist, not an Italian, and certainly not a Venetian. They will be reburied in the chamber in which they have slept for five hundred years."

"How do you know it was five hundred years? Maybe it was just fifty, or twenty-five. Maybe it was just last year."

"Come on now, Maggie. Don't give me that attitude. I've gotten enough from everyone else. The reason I know it was around five hundred years is a legal document we found that mentions a man by the name of Claudius Vincus. His nickname was 'Lingua Malus,' the words on the wall in the chamber."

"What does 'Lingua Malus' mean?"

"It literally means 'bad tongue.' According to the old document, Vincus was a procurer of young women. He was arrested and placed on trial to appease the pope and other religious dignitaries in one of their visits to Venice. Vincus was charged with what you would call pimping today. His girls were never found, but he was sentenced to two months in prison. After only two weeks in his cell, he hanged himself. We believe that he had hidden the young women in the chamber of the clock tower, planning to return there and free them after the trial. He may have thought that he would be found innocent and would be released if the court could not find the girls. The young woman who was pregnant may have been his sister. We also believe that Lingua Malus could mean 'liar.' No one would have known that the young women were in the chamber except perhaps his brother, who visited him in prison just before he hanged himself. His brother was a stonemason who did repair work in the piazza. Stone had been placed over the ancient door and had concealed the entryway for hundreds of years. Since Venice flooded so often, they may have drowned."

"What you are saying, then, is that the women died accidentally?"

"Yes, Maggie. They most likely did."

Lingua Malus, Lingua Malus, she thought. Did it also mean liar, liar? Maggie spoke sharply to Eduardo. "Even more reason to remove them from the tower, wouldn't you think?"

"Not necessarily. You see the public has gotten wind of this. Inquiries are coming from all over the world. People wish to see the chamber in which the young women died. We'll return them to the location where they have slept for five hundred years. We've installed a glass window in the floor of the tower, and visitors will come from everywhere to see their tomb. No new monument has been added to San Marcos in hundreds of years. Some company even wants to make a movie about their lives. Thousands and thousands of tourists will visit here to see the young women's tomb, and they will spend a lot of money."

Maggie looked at him for a long moment and realized, regrettably, that he was probably right. She, on the other hand, was wrong in her earlier assessment. He had changed a lot more than she thought he had. Was it pressure from others in the government? Was he just interested in being a "yes" man, something he had never seemed to be years ago. Of course, she reasoned, he was a married man now with a family to support, but he was the one who had called her, not the other way around. Maybe, he had simply wanted her expertise on the project and she had totally misread their conversations. Once again, she admitted she was really bad at reading signals from men.

Eduardo hurried to the tower to get help with the boxes. He returned with several young men and they quickly removed all of the boxes from the boat. They practically ran to the tower as though afraid of their cargo.

"Hey, you guys, slow down," Maggie shouted, but

they ignored her. She noticed that one of the boxes was coming apart. It must have been jostled during shipment. She could imagine bones all over the square and the media frenzy that would lead to. She hurried after the young men, anxious to finish the task without incident and get back to the real world.

Maggie entered the portal and cautiously made her way down the darkened passageway for what she knew would be the final time. As she stepped into the chamber, a young man set down the last box with a thud. It split open at the corner and he backed away.

"It's O.K." she said, "I'll handle this." She pulled some packing tape from her bag and began to retape the box. Once more she caught the unmistakable odor of something dead. As she shifted the box to lift it and place it on top of the one next to it, something fell out. She picked it up, studied it for a long moment, then placed it back in the small slit at the corner of the box. She then added another piece of packing tape.

Maggie stood there watching the men as they hurried to finish. They were enclosing the young victims in a brick tomb inside the chamber. A glass viewing window had been placed in a hollowed out area of the floor above. People were probably lining up outside to get the first peek. They would be disappointed if they had come to see corpses strewn about.

She climbed the stairs, exited the campanile, and saw Eduardo standing off to the side, studying his hands. Why do men always study their hands when they feel guilty about something? He knew she did not like this, but he was right. It really was none of her business. She would be on the next plane out of town, and he would live the rest of his life with these people. She would finish her final report on the analysis of the women's remains and send it to Eduardo. It would end up gathering dust on a bookcase deep in the archives. So much for justice. She walked up to Eduardo, and he smiled at her. Oh, that smile. She didn't smile back. "Goodbye, Eduardo. It was great to see you again. I appreciate the opportunity to do the analysis on these remains. I know how hard you must have worked to get it cleared through the government agencies." Eduardo looked at Maggie for what seemed like a very long moment. She used one finger to gently lift a small lock of hair from his forehead, a gesture she often had made in the past. She willed herself to keep memories of their college days behind the wall she had built to separate herself from disappointment. Turning, she walked toward the small boat, her ride back to reality.

As Maggie settled into her seat on the plane at Marco Polo Airport, she thought about Eduardo. Sometimes the past is best left in the past. She knew she might never hear from him again. As the plane taxied down the runway, she also thought about the damaged box and how she had chosen not to tell Eduardo what she had picked up from the floor in the tower chamber. The item she had placed back into the box was an upper right canine with a peculiar inverted "v" notched into its biting surface. Was there an extra set of bones in the chamber on the piazza?

Chapter 12

The phone was ringing, and Maggie didn't want to answer it. She was ready to jerk it out of the wall. It had been two days since her return from Venice. She wanted to rest for a while before facing Lucas. Besides, the jet lag seemed to affect her more than usual this time. She just couldn't go back to the morgue yet, though she needed to look at the canal cases and provide some final opinions for Browning. She decided to answer the phone because at 10 p.m., she knew it was probably one of the three local men in her life. Jimmy wanting some kind of update on the feature story he was writing about the Venetian women, Lucas wanting to know if everything had gone all right, or Dan wanting to know when she was coming back to work. Those three were the only ones who had the gall to call her that late at night. Even Rodney Durham wouldn't be so bold.

It was Lucas. "Maggie, could you come over to Maura's house?"

"It's late. Can't it wait until tomorrow?"

"No. Please come now, as fast as you can. I have something to show you. You will only believe it if you see it for yourself."

"I'll be there in a little bit."

"Maggie."

"Yeah?"

"I didn't know about any of this. I swear."

"Lucas, what in the world are you talking about? I can't take many more surprises."

"Just get here fast."

"Where is 'here'? I don't know where Maura lives—I mean lived." He gave her the address on Second Street. "I'm on my way," she said.

Now what in the world could Lucas be talking about? She really didn't want to see him yet because she hadn't decided what to do about something that might now rest in a chamber thousands of miles from home.

Maggie edged her car up next to the curb in front of Maura's house. A light on the side was on, but the front was dark. The old mansion looked intimidating with just the streetlight to illuminate its eggplant color. But Lucas must have been watching for her. The front door opened quickly, startling her as she hurried up the walk.

"Maggie, thank God you're here. Come inside." His unshaven face and weary eyes suggested more than one sleepless night.

"Lucas, what's going on that you had to drag me all the way over here at this time of night?"

"Come with me." They made their way through the house past ancient mirrors and armoires, windows covered with lace and velvet, past scents of orange blossoms and lilac. Their footfalls were silent, the normal sounds muffled by thick carpets laid end to end down the darkened hall. The house felt old and dead. Lucas led her to a small room at the back.

"For goodness sake, Lucas, this is creepy and I've been creeped enough lately."

"Just a second, Maggie. You have to see for yourself. Otherwise, you're not going to believe it. I thought the door to this room was just a door to the outside that was permanently locked. I didn't realize until yesterday that it led to another room. I hadn't paid any attention to it until I decided to walk around outside. Something about the walls didn't add up. You know how I always want to map everything."

He turned on the light, and Maggie stepped back. She could see herself everywhere. Pictures of her, newspaper articles about her, pictures of her projects, even pictures in Venice. She didn't understand. Obviously, neither Lucas nor Maggie knew Maura Stone.

"O.K., Lucas. Start from the beginning and tell me why my picture has been used to wallpaper this room."

"Maggie, I don't know the whole story. What I do know is that Maura had another name."

"What?"

"Her real name was Galilee Bunch."

"Galilee Bunch? That doesn't sound European."

"European?"

"She told me she grew up in Europe."

"Well, that's not exactly true. I think she was from a place called Mercy, Arkansas. Here's a stack of old letters from someone named Viola Bunch asking for money. I believe she was Maura's mother."

"Was?"

"I get the impression she's dead."

"Oh, well, so Maura lied about where she came from. So what? We all have secrets."

"That's not the important part. I think she knew the women in the canals."

"What? How?"

"Look at this." He picked up a worn, leather-bound notebook. In it were pages and pages of dated entries and small sketches. Some of the drawings were circles with symbols in the center. They looked all too familiar. Lucas continued. "The only body from the canals that I saw was the accountant's, but didn't she have a tattoo like this drawing?" He was pointing to a small circle with a lightning rod in it.

Maggie nodded. "Yes."

"Do these drawings resemble the other tattoos?" he said, pointing to small circles here and there throughout the book.

"You could say that," she replied, dumbstruck. "Lucas, I don't understand."

"I don't either, but have you ever heard of the Clearwater Hotel in Hot Springs, Arkansas?"

"No."

"Well, I think part of the answer is there. Maggie, would you go to the Clearwater tomorrow and check it out while I go through the rest of this journal and sift through these other papers?"

"Well, I guess I could, but why am I plastered all over these walls like bathroom paper?"

"That I don't know for sure. But when I first met Maura you were all she could ever talk about, something about your being the 'savior of lost souls.'"

"That's rich. How am I the savior of lost souls? I don't even know how to save my own."

"Well, that I don't know either, but every time a body was found in the canals, Maura would mumble something about baptism and how the women were cleansed of any sins they may have committed. She said you were the person who could put them to rest because she knew that sooner or later you would get them identified. One time she said that your track record was too good to leave the women unidentified for long."

"Well, Lucas, didn't you find any of that even the slightest bit kooky?"

"A little, but she was very religious, Maggie, and she never missed a chance to attend church. She was particularly interested in confession, though she admitted that she wasn't raised as a Catholic."

"Probably not, if she's from Mercy, Arkansas. I would guess piney woods Baptist. I don't get it."

"Neither do it, but I think the Clearwater can help us. Will you go?" How could she refuse? Besides, she was more than a little troubled that, even indirectly, she might be a link to the women in the canals.

"I'll go, Lucas, but when I get back we have some serious things to talk about, not the least of which is Maura's—I mean Galilee's—cremation."

Lucas looked down at his hands. Maggie's suspicions were stronger. Maura Stone, alias Galilee Bunch, might now reside in the bowels of a clock tower in Venice, Italy.

Maggie pulled into a parking lot at the Clearwater about 4:30 p.m. the next day. A few people wandered up and down the gallery and only briefly glanced her way as she took the steps two at a time. She wanted the whole thing over and done with.

The friendly young man at the registration desk listened with patient disinterest as she described how she was looking for someone. He wasn't particularly attentive until Maggie showed him a picture of Maura. His eyes brightened as he spoke.

"Why, that's Miss Galilee. She's a regular here at the baths."

"The baths?"

"Yeah, third floor up. Go look for yourself. Ask to speak to Oberon. She'll help you."

The old hotel had seen better days, but Maggie understood how enticing the baths might be. The few women who were still in the bathhouse seemed to be lingering there, not wanting to leave.

"I'm looking for Oberon," she said generally to everyone. A tall, regal, black woman came toward her.

"I'm Oberon. What do you want?"

Her voice had a wonderful lyrical quality to it, perhaps Caribbean in origin. It sounded familiar, a little like the unusual accent Maggie often had heard in Maura's voice.

"Oberon, my name is Maggie Andrepont. I'm with the coroner's office in New Orleans. Do you know this woman?" Maggie showed her the snapshot of Maura with Lucas in Venice.

"Of course, I know her. That's Miss Galilee. She's been coming to the baths for more than twenty years. She's very special."

"What about this woman?" Maggie had pulled out the photo of the Jane Doe with the scar on her chin and the short cropped hair.

"Oh, Jesse, my sweet girl. But she looks dead."

"She is. So is Galilee."

"What do you mean?" she said, sinking into a near-by chair. "Miss Galilee will be here any day now. She was supposed to come last week, but she didn't. But she'll be here. She can't be dead. And what about Jesse? She's not even in New Orleans. She left here months ago for Philadelphia."

Maggie hated to pose the next question. "Oberon, do you know any other young women who have left here without notice in the last couple of years?"

"Well, there was Francine, but she was an odd one. Always insisting her toenails and fingernails be perfect, saying that Miss Galilee said if your nails were perfect you could look at them and know your heart was pure, no matter what went on with your body and your life. She's been gone a year or more. But she's an orphan, so nobody really cares."

"Anyone else?" Maggie asked, relentlessly.

"Maybe one more, but she's not right in the head. She also ain't too pretty, Little Nadina. Young. Short, stubby little thing. She followed Miss Galilee around all over the place begging her to do her fingernails and toe-nails, too, so she could look pretty like Miss Galilee."

"That's odd. Galilee was a client here and wanted to paint the helper's nails?"

"Oh, she loved nails. She learned to do that when she was young back wherever she came from. Said she used to do her mama's nails all the time. All the helpers love Miss Galilee. What happened to her?" she asked, her voice catching.

"She drowned."

"Now wait a minute. Miss Galilee don't swim. She don't even get into the water, except the baths."

"What about tattoos?"

"Tattoos? What are you talking about?"

"Did Jesse, or Francine, or Nadina have tattoos?"

"I don't know. I never saw tattoos, but who knows? I never saw them naked, neither."

"Do Jesse and Nadina's parents live around here?"

"Just up Ellerberry Road. Are you gonna be telling Nadina's mama something bad, too?"

"I'm afraid so." Maggie turned and walked out of the bathhouse, heading toward the stairs to the lobby. She could hear a loud wail rising from the bath area. Her head was reeling as she walked up to the registration desk with one more question for the bored young clerk. "Where are the local sheriff's office and Ellerberry Road?"

Around 8:00 p.m. Maggie headed back to Little Rock to catch the red-eye to New Orleans. Computer enhancements of the three unidentified victims would not be necessary. They were going home to Arkansas. She only hoped that Lucas had had good luck sorting through Maura's papers and that they could provide them with information to fill in the gaps. The picture was getting more and more complex, but what was becoming increasingly clear was that Maura Stone had more than a little to do with the women in the canals. And the tattoos must mean something, though it didn't really matter if Maura had branded the girls or not.

Lucas was waiting for Maggie at the airport. He knew she had left her car in short-term parking, so she assumed he had something important to tell her.

"Any luck in Hot Springs?"

"Like you wouldn't believe. Maura's real name *was* Galilee Bunch. She's probably from Arkansas like you thought. She had a weird fetish for doing nails, and, though you're not ready for this, I think she killed those girls in the canals. Also, the latest victim is Nadina Jones, fresh out of Hot Springs, Arkansas, and until a few months ago an employee at the Clearwater bathhouse. Same for the fourth victim we found, the pretty young black woman, except the timing is a little different. Her name is Jesse Robertson, and her parents identified her from the photo I took when Sidney pulled her out of the canal. Her parents knew that it was Jesse instantly, even down to the scar on her chin. She worked at the Clearwater until a little more than a year ago when she left suddenly, saying she was moving to Philadelphia. She and her parents weren't really close. They decided that she just didn't want to stay in touch with them. The last unidentified one is Francine, an orphan. She was the second body found in the canal."

"You learned all that in one day?"

"Yep. The Clearwater is quite a little hotbed of information, and it seems that Maura was going there for more than just the baths. She was most likely recruiting these young women. If I had to guess, Lucas, I would say that she was a madam and the young women were her prostitutes."

"You may be right, Maggie. And the tattoos are no longer a mystery either."

"You found out something about the tattoos?"

"Yes, Maura was tattooing the young women who worked for her."

"For heaven's sake, why?"

"Two reasons, I think. For one, she had a burn scar on one of her own fingers."

"I remember that from the autopsy."

"Well, looking through her journal, I've found more than one reference to it and that it was a reminder of how she had been tortured as a child. She once told me that someone her mother knew had put it there. That's all she ever said. She let me look closely at it one day. It looked like a cigarette burn or something like that. She said it was a reminder to never let any man get the best of her again. I believe she tattooed her girls for the same reason. Always keep the upper hand."

"What did the symbols mean?"

"I'm not sure. But they may have something to do with the four elements of the universe. She was interested in Germanic runes."

"Oh, you mean pictographs?"

"Yes, something like that. She was always sketching different symbols and making up her own.

"Such as?"

"You know, symbols for earth, wind, fire, and water."

"Why those?"

"She talked about them a lot and how natural forces could shape a person's destiny."

"Well, isn't that ironic. It was water that killed her. What was the other reason for the tattoos? You said there were two."

"Well, this may be just a hunch, but Jimmy O'Malley came by yesterday with some interesting information. He can be quite resourceful. He said that he knew one of the women, the last one found. Didn't you say her name was Nadina? Jimmy called her Sadie."

"Yes, her real name is Nadina. What did Jimmy say?"

"He said that he met her and spent some time with her until he found out how young she was. She had a special tattoo. She told him if he could find the tattoo on her body in a minute or less, he earned the right to certain special privileges with her. Hidden in plain view, you might say." Maggie thought about how Jimmy loved games.

"Why didn't Jimmy come forward before now?"

"Simple. He only recently got to see the morgue shot of the girl. She was the only one he knew. He never met the others."

"But, Lucas, why did Maura kill them?"

"I think she did it because she just couldn't go on with that life anymore. She also didn't want me to know that she had been a prostitute and a madam."

"Don't you think that is a little conceited, to think that she would kill for you?"

"I know it sounds that way, Maggie." Lucas sighed deeply and shook his head. "But I think she really did love me and thought that I would hate her if I found out about what she did for a living. That must be why she wouldn't have sex with me." Now Maggie knew the reason why he was so touchy when she asked him in Venice if he was sleeping with Maura.

"Well, forget the 'why' for the moment. How did she do it?"

"Speaking of that, Yancy finished his analysis on the material you found on one of the cases. It's nineteenth-century brick. Maura has a pile of them in her backyard. The women trusted her. She must have surprised them all."

"Lucas, one more question, and then I'm going home. How do I fit into all of this?"

"Hero worship."

"Right. Some hero I am."

"Seriously, she spoke highly of you. I believe she got the idea to put the women in the canals after the first one floated up."

"What do you mean, after the first one? Aren't they all her victims?"

"I guess so, but the first one isn't like the others."

"Tell me something I don't know."

"I'm still working on that."

"Lucas, I want to go home."

"O.K, Maggie, I'm sorry. I didn't mean to keep you here so long, but we have to tell Dan and Dr. Browning about all of this first thing in the morning."

"You haven't told them already?"

"No, I wanted to tell you first."

"Let's get out of here, Lucas. I need to see you tomorrow anyway." Lucas pushed Maura's journal toward her.

"Here, Maggie."

"What's this for?"

"I want you to read it."

"Why?"

"Please just read some of it. I think you should."

"Oh, Lucas, I would feel like I was trespassing."

"But who better than you to read it? She respected you."

"I might read some of it," she agreed reluctantly.

Chapter 13

Maggie settled down into bed with a large cup of coffee. Her curiosity had gotten the best of her. The coffee should keep her from falling asleep until she had read at least a portion of Maura's journal. She really did want to try to understand her.

She opened the well-worn cover of the little leather book and flipped through a few of the pages. Then she returned to the beginning, picking out excerpts here and there as she turned the pages.

In this book, I will write my life.

I guess I don't know what to say. No one else will ever read this. Maybe I can say things I've wanted to say for a long time. Maybe I can make the dreams go away.

When men look at me, I feel so many different things. I like that they find me attractive, but sometimes I hate them and I hate myself for liking them. They just want to take off my clothes and do the things they do. Why shouldn't they have to pay for it? Nothing is free. I learned that a long time ago. What is that saying Mama used to have? "The milk may be free but the hand on the teat is gonna cost you."

Tonight was a busy night. Eight is pretty much a record. My skin is dry from all those baths. The work on the front porch is paid for now. The swing will go at the northern end. I miss that old swing on Mama's porch. If I swung it just right, its squeaking covered up the sounds coming from her room.

Maggie skipped several entries.

I like the new picket fence out front. It says, 'This is where a happy person lives.' Its boards are pointed at the top, like pitchforks.

Oh, Lord, the man came today with an estimate to replace the kitchen cabinets. They will have to wait. I guess I could try to bring in another helper, but Mama always said the smart bird never shares the nest.

Thumbing through the pages, Maggie spotted Lucas's name.

I met a man today. He's different. Lucas is his name. He has sad eyes. It's raining hard outside. Time to get out the buckets.

144

I took a walk down to the Quarter this morning. I love all the strangers. They all seem so happy down there. Some of the artists were drawing cartoon faces. I don't think they look like the people they are supposed to be. They are like Mardi Gras masks. I don't like them. Some girl was dressed like an angel and just stood really still while people took pictures of her. I didn't like her at all.

I saw Lucas again today. L U C A S. He seems real. He is kind.

September 5. I can't keep up the payments on this house. Maybe I should just get rid of it. The termites have come back and the back porch has started sagging in the middle again. Stupid sewer. I know it's to blame. I love my house. It's over a hundred fifty years old. I just want to curl up in my bed and go to sleep.

October 12. Esau's letter came today. He must have found my address on some of Mama's old letters. He's not getting one more dime from me.

November 20. It's almost Thanksgiving. Maybe I'll buy a turkey breast and a can of cranberry sauce. I bet the leaves are turning gold and brown back home. I may have to sell my last chandelier. That man from the antique store has been slinking around again.

November 30. Jesse arrives tomorrow. I'll put her in the spare room up front and she can hang her clothes in the cherry armoire. Someone needs to use it before I have to sell it, too. That room needs a good cleaning.

It's been shut up for years and I know there's dust everywhere. Jesse can use the hall bath.

Maggie skipped several pages and came to another one that mentioned Lucas.

Lucas Delacroix Evans. What am I going to do with you? You showed up last night with a muffuletta sandwich and a bottle of wine. No one has ever brought me a muffuletta before. We sat on the porch swing til 9 and I had to ask you to leave. I couldn't tell you why.

March 14. Francine is giving me problems. She won't wear proper clothes and she doesn't bathe enough. She thinks the tattoo is stupid and isn't interested in her nails anymore. I think she would like to go out on her own. I should have left her at the baths.

May 25. Little Nadina. I wonder why I brought you here. You are the sweetest of them all. I will rot in hell for this.

Maggie skipped over several other pages where Maura berated herself over and over. She thumbed backward in the journal looking for even a small notation about the accountant or Dorothy Brown. She found part of what she was looking for.

Betty is not working out. She's better in the books than in bed and cries every time someone touches her below the waist. I just have to decide what I am going to do. I don't even like her particularly. I confess that I am not godly and I do not walk the straight and narrow path of God.

Several paragraphs later Maggie saw something even more disturbing.

The nightmares have come back. Sometimes I am so afraid.

Another entry drew Maggie toward it.

Lucas let me help him in the laboratory he shares with Maggie. Signs of her were all around. In a different place, we could have been friends. I could help her with the girls from the canals.

"I bet you could," Maggie said to herself. She continued reading. Page after page was filled with references to Maura's house on Second Street, to the young women she had brought to New Orleans, and to Maggie.

Maggie's favorite color must be blue. She wears it a lot. The color of sky suits her well.

Maggie was about to put the book down for the night, but a side of Maura was beginning to emerge that might explain her actions, partially. She thumbed through some of the last pages and stopped when she saw Lucas's name again.

I love Lucas. There. I've said it. I love you, Lucas. I love you.

I am running out of money. I don't know what to do. Esau is calling every day. Only Nadina remains, and she is afraid of me. Little flower, Nadina. Soon, I will make you some of my special tea. With God in heaven you will thank me if I take you away from this wicked, unforgiving world. You are washed in the blood, in the soul-cleansing blood of the Lamb.

This house is dark and voices whisper to me from behind the curtains. Madam Eva read my palm last night in the Quarter. She would not tell me what my life line showed. I ran from her booth when she laid out her Tarot cards. I saw the death card.

July 1. I am going to Venice, Italy, with Lucas. I have never been so happy in my entire life. My will is in my lawyer's hands. His name is Winston Thibodeaux.

Maggie couldn't read anymore. The little she had read disturbed her. It seemed strange and disjointed, like someone who flirted with shadows. Someone tormented, someone afraid. She could not believe she was feeling sorry for a killer.

She laid Maura's journal on the bedside table and closed her eyes, trying to go to sleep. It was well past midnight. She tossed and turned, got up and drank water, then tried warm milk. She gave the bulk of the milk to Tango who made short work of it. She decided to go to the lab, wanting to piece some things together. Something wasn't adding up.

It was almost 1 a.m. when Maggie pulled into the parking lot at the morgue. The parking lot was well lit but she hurried into the morgue at a brisker pace than usual. She was getting extremely jumpy these days but felt that much of the search to catch the murderer was over. Just a few loose ends needed tying up.

She sat down at her desk. She started flipping through the files again. If Maura thought she could save the women by identifying them and giving them back a sense of dignity, where did she get the idea in the first place? After the first death? Dorothy Brown. Back to Dorothy again. Something wasn't right. Dorothy was not like the other ones, and she had that cinder block tied to her.

Maggie mulled over the cases for almost an hour, going back and forth from one to the other. Everything was just a little too neat, a little too wet. What was Maura's intent? Cleaning house so that she could be with Lucas? Perhaps, but what about Dorothy Brown? Was she one of Maura's girls? She definitely was the only one with a cinder block. If Maura had meant for her to float up for Maggie to help identify her, why would she have tied a cinder block to her leg? Something dawned on Maggie. She hadn't seen any mention of Dorothy's name in Maura's journal. Maybe she had just missed it. She glanced at the clock on the wall. 1:45 a.m. "This is ridiculous. Go home, Maggie. Are you trying to kill yourself from exhaustion?"

Maggie had just put away the files and laid out a few scalpels and scissors for the burn victim that had arrived while she was gone when she heard something at the lab door. She froze, almost gagging from the fear rising in her throat. She had forgotten to lock the deadbolt. She listened for a terrifying moment, and the sound went away. Still alert and very uneasy, she moved quietly and slowly toward the door, her eyes on the deadbolt.

Just a few more steps. She was almost there when the lock clicked and the door flew open with a bang. Sidney entered the lab, the grin of a demented soul stretched across his face. Maggie's heart pounded. He appeared to be drunk or on drugs and was reeling back and forth.

"Here's the file you been wanting, Maggie," he said, throwing a manila folder at her feet. He stood there, a short rope dangling from his left hand. He began tying and untying the ends of the rope with the methodical skill of a beached sailor. His eyes were wild. A little drool slipped from the corner of his mouth. Maggie watched the drool slide down his chin and onto the floor.

Trying to calm him, she spoke softly, "Sidney? How did you know that I had a file missing?"

"What do you think, slut? I took it from your car. I tried to put it back in your house but that damned dog of yours kept me from breaking the lock on your front door."

Maggie's throat constricted from the pain of a silent scream locked inside. She slowly backed against the examining table. The scalpels she had just laid out were inches from her right hand. If Sidney saw her pick up a scalpel, how would he react? She needed to distract him. "Sidney, what's wrong with you? Why would you want Dorothy Brown's file?"

"Nothing's wrong with me. It's what's going to be wrong with you. You know I killed Dorothy Brown. I've seen it in your eyes." His hands never stopped moving with the rope. Maggie's greatest fear was that the rope was meant for her.

"Sidney, what are you talking about?" she said desperately, her throat aching to scream for someone, anyone.

"Shut up, slut. I'm doing the talking now. You pretend to be so interested in me, concerned about me.

150

'How's your head, Sidney? Seen a doctor lately, Sidney?' Gettin' inside my head. That's what you've been doing. I used to think you were the most beautiful woman in the world, but you're just a piece of trash who takes off her clothes for a dollar a dance." Maggie's sharp intake of breath surprised even her. She ignored his remark. She needed to calm him.

"Sidney, just relax. Everything will be O.K."

"Relax nothing. I didn't mean to kill Dorothy. I swear it was an accident. I just put a little too much pressure on her neck and then she wouldn't wake up. We were having sex. You know about selling sex, don't you, Maggie? Or maybe I should say, 'Spider Rose,' your dance name at the White Swan in the old days. I thought you were so beautiful and I saw it then."

"What are you talking about, Sidney?"

"The rose tattoo, with a spider crawling up it. I was sittin' at the bar. I saw it real close. I also saw those two guys fighting over you. I wanted to touch you so bad, touch your spider."

"Sidney, you're not making any sense. Let's talk about Dorothy."

"I don't want to talk about Dorothy. She just sort of went to sleep. I didn't know what to do with her. So I tied a block to her and threw her in the canal. I didn't think she'd come up. But I didn't have nothing to do with those other women, I swear. I know who did, though. I watched her do one. I saw her put that last girl in the canal and I saw her slip and fall in. I think she saw me too as she bobbed up and down like a cork. I didn't take a step to help her. I just thought, 'Goodbye, devil woman.'"

"Sidney, we know, too. We think she killed the other women."

"Lies, always lies."

Sidney edged closer to Maggie and she saw the wildness in his eyes. She probably couldn't reach him, but she tried, speaking as calmly as she could. "Sidney, do you want to go with me to see Dan and let him get help for you, the headaches and all? You know Dan likes you and respects you."

"No." He jumped forward.

Maggie fought to keep from fainting. She was alone in a morgue with a madman. No one even knew she was there, and she had to get out. Her right hand was still behind her. It closed around a scalpel handle. She picked it up just as Sidney lunged at her with the rope. She raked the blade across his left cheek as he tried to grab her throat. He screamed and leaped back. Maggie moved like she hadn't moved in years, out the door, down the hall, and through the entrance, hitting the silent police call on the alarm system as she went. She made it as far as the parking lot where her car stood all alone.

She struggled to open her car door, knowing full well that her keys were back in the lab. Sidney quickly came up behind her, the crunching sounds of his shoes on the shell-covered parking lot like bones being crushed in the jaws of a rabid animal. He grabbed her neck with his arm, bringing her to her knees as he tore at her blouse with his free hand. She struggled helplessly to loosen his hold on her. He wrapped the rope around her neck, tightening it. The buttons popped from her blouse as she struggled helplessly. Sidney tore at her pants. He was panting and pushed her down on the hood of the car, increasing the pressure on the rope. His lips almost touched hers. He flattened them against Maggie's and the little breathing space she had left was lost. A sour taste of blood, old wine, and cigarettes filled her senses as green and red stars burst into flames in her head. Someone seemed to be screaming. She felt the world go black.

Maggie was cold and it hurt to breathe. A voice kept urging her to try. The voice was familiar, encircling her, warming her like a worn, soft blanket. Finally, she could open her eyes. She tried to adjust them to the lights shining all around. She was in the back seat of a vehicle and it was moving. Her upper body was cradled in someone's lap, someone speaking quietly and steadily to her. When she could focus, she realized it was Dan. He looked worried but forced a smile when she tried to talk. Nothing but grunts came from her throat.

"It's O.K., Maggie. Don't try to talk," he said, awkwardly trying to rearrange her clothes. "We've got Sidney. We think he's the serial murderer. He keeps rambling about Dorothy Brown. You must have hit the silent alarm. The police called me on their way here. I knew something was wrong. Thank God you're all right. There was blood everywhere. I thought you were cut, but it's just Sidney's blood."

All she could do was shake her head, trying to suck in as much air as possible to revive her oxygen-starved brain. Reluctant tears slipped from her eyes as they arrived at the hospital and Dan began to lift her.

"Come on, Maggie, you need to be checked out by a doctor." She tried to protest but nothing came out. She was just glad to be alive and thankful that Sidney had been arrested. What he said about Dorothy Brown and how she was the only one he killed placed a major piece into an almost finished puzzle. She couldn't help but remember the other things he had said.

Chapter 14

Dan insisted that Maggie stay overnight in the hospital. She decided maybe he was right. She might get a little undisturbed sleep.

By noon her eyes were wide open. The corridors in the hospital were quiet. All Maggie knew was that she was starving for some shrimp and crab gumbo, or crawfish bisque, or just about anything with seafood in it. A light knock at the door was a welcome sound. Whoever it was could give her a ride home. She was ditching this place before dark. It was Lucas.

"Lucas. Boy, am I glad to see you," Maggie croaked.

"Dan called me and told me what happened. I would die if something happened to you, Maggie." His voice wavered as he spoke.

"Hey, now, don't you go soft on me, or we'll both be crying. We're the tough ones, remember, the survivors."

"Why didn't you go straight home last night? I would have gone to the morgue with you if I had known you wanted to go there."

"I did go home. I just didn't stay. I read some of Maura's journal and then I couldn't sleep. So I went to the morgue. But can you do me a favor? Can you get me out of here? I want to go home now."

"Well, Maggie, I could, but I think we'd both be in trouble if I did. It's Dan. He's waiting outside to see you and has told the staff you are to spend the night, even if they have to restrain you. I think they also have your clothes."

"That man. How dare he? Well, when you leave, could you call Moses and ask him to take care of Brutus and Tango for me tonight? He knows their routine better than anybody. In fact, I think they like him more than they like me."

"I doubt that, Maggie. Sounds like you are feeling a little sorry for yourself, but, of course, I'll call him."

"Lucas." He shifted uncomfortably, knowing by the tone in Maggie's scratchy voice what was coming next. The question she had been saving for a better time just popped out. "How and why did Maura's canine tooth end up in the boxes holding the bones of the Venetian women? Is the rest of her there, too?" The look on his face revealed the truth.

"Yes. All of her bones are there. They are intermingled among the Venetian women's bones, and her soft tissue has been incinerated."

"What about her skull?"

"It's in one of the boxes, too, camouflaged under some packing foam. The box was a little overpacked."

That's what Maggie had smelled coming from the boxes on more than one occasion. Even after bones are cleaned, the smell of death lingers.

"Well, that must be why the box split open in Venice."

"What?" he stammered, his face pale.

"Don't worry. Only one tooth fell out. If it had been any other tooth, I might not have paid much attention to it. But, when I saw it, I knew immediately that it was hers. That canine has always struck me as unusual, with that inverted 'v' chipped out of it. You know that's what we get paid for, Lucas, to be observant. Since it was damaged, the nerve was probably dead and part of the root must have dissolved, which would make it very fragile. But I thought she wanted her whole body cremated. That's what you told me."

"I'm sorry, Maggie. I lied to you."

"Yes, you did, and I need to know why."

"Well, I knew you would never have gone along with the idea of putting her with the other women, but she talked so much about how beautiful Venice was, how she was so happy there, how she wished we could stay there forever. I cared about her, Maggie, in a way I find hard to explain. Not like Amy, but at one point I did feel as though I could fall in love with her. I know now that wasn't the case. I don't know if you can understand this, but I felt that she was infinitely sad. I just wanted to make things better."

"Lucas, she was something of a serial killer."

"I don't think I would call her that."

"Then what would you call her? Benefactor? Judge, jury, and executioner? I'm quite sure those girls never dreamed that their savior would murder them. That must be how she surprised them with the bricks upside the head."

"I don't think she saw it that way. I think she thought she was saving them."

"From what?"

"From her and from what inevitably would have happened to them if she had to make them leave. Life on the streets is short and terminal in this town. Nobody cares about prostitutes, especially old prostitutes, and you're worn out at thirty if you're still alive. Look at their murder rate and then look at the arrest rate of their killers."

"Well, I still don't think anyone has the right to kill for any reason, but it's too late for all of them now. What about Maura? Do you think her death was an accident or suicide?"

"I think it was an accident. She couldn't swim, and I think she fell into the canal when she tried to dump Nadina."

"One more question, Lucas. Something that's really bothering me. How in the world did you get her bones cleaned so fast?"

"Well, if you really want to know, the first night I removed all of the tissue, working till 5 a.m. the next day. You had left a note saying that you would be out, so I just kept going."

"I shutter to think how you could do that to someone with whom you had been so close."

"I closed my mind, you know, like you do sometimes when we're working on children. After a while, she became just another set of bones."

Unfortunately, Maggie knew exactly what he meant. She thought she was the only one who did that.

"Anyway," he continued, "I put her bones in the hot water whirlpool bath as I went along, added a half gallon of the degreaser, and turned the heat gauge to high. By the end of the day, the tissue just melted away, like a boiled chicken."

"You put clean, white bones in with the Venetian women's bones?"

"No, I dried the bones as best I could under the fume hood and then dyed them with brown shoe polish. They looked very similar to the five-hundred-year-old bones after that. Then I put a few of her bones in each box."

"So that's why you wanted to box the bones yourself. You knew I would know if even one bone didn't belong in those boxes."

"Yes, I knew, Maggie, and I kept it from you, and I also knew that you might hate me for it."

"Of course I don't hate you, but how did you think you could ever get away with this?"

"I almost did."

"Where do we go from here, Lucas? You've lied to me. You have probably committed some international crime by transporting Maura's body across the ocean, and it will certainly rankle the Italians if they ever learn about this. In the process, you also may have jeopardized any possibility of my ever getting work in Europe again."

"This is not all lost on me, Maggie."

"Is this justice to you, Lucas?"

"No, it's a tragedy. Maura ends up with the very kind of women she was trying to escape, and the whole thing turns into a fiasco that could destroy the one true friendship I have in this world. I know it was wrong, but I probably would do it again. She was a victim, too, Maggie, and I've seen too many victims lately."

"Go home, Lucas. I have to think about all of this. My throat is killing me, and I'm probably very lucky to be alive. Not much else matters right now."

"Dan is outside. Do you want me to send him in?"

"Not yet. I need to speak to him, but could you ask him to give me just a few minutes?" He nodded and quickly slipped from the room.

Maggie's mind shifted to Sidney and how he had raved about the White Swan. Then her thoughts turned to Dan. He had saved her last night. It was not the first time. She thought about how he looked the night she met him. He had literally saved her life that time too. She was seventeen and had run away from home when her mother died, ending up in the White Swan, the seediest strip joint in the French Quarter. It was her third night as a stripper on the bar. She hadn't wanted to do it, but she was starving. She was also under age and the guy at the White Swan was the only one who would hire her. He told her to lie about her age. Even though she was as skinny as a fourteen-year-old, he thought the customers might like a change from the usual busty group. One in particular liked it a lot. He had climbed onto the bar with his fists full of dollars, trying to stuff them into Maggie's garter. She was scared to death and started screaming.

All at once he was not the only person on the bar. From nowhere, a huge, gawky, young man ran through the open front door, jumped onto the bar, and took down the troublemaker. Dan. He and some friends had been walking through the Quarter when he heard her screams. He was waiting for Maggie at the exit that night and asked if she wanted to go for coffee. They talked until sunup. She told him about her dream to go to college. Dan listened intently, the first person other than her mother who ever did.

"I have an idea," he said. Maggie would never forget those words. He took her back to the room she had rented in the flophouse, the Dover, and told her to pack her bags. She had little to pack. They drove to Mid City, where he dropped her at a small house. The next day he returned and took her to register for her first college classes, insisting on lending her the money for two semesters. It was weeks before she found out that he was the new upstart coroner everyone was talking about, and more than three years before she could pay back the loan, but she did. He owned the house in Mid City, and though she felt guilty for accepting his generosity, she stayed there for over a year until she could get her own place.

Dan never asked her to go to bed with him, but some two years after they met, she did, perhaps out of gratitude more than anything. It was pleasant enough. He was the first. She wasn't really ready for a serious relationship. Neither was he. Before they knew it, she had graduated and left for Arizona, where she met Eduardo. When she got back to New Orleans, she was still smarting from the loss of Eduardo. But even he faded from memory as her archaeology business began to take off and require fifteen-hour days. The only reminders of Eduardo were the endless flowers he sent every year.

During a conversation with Dan one day, he asked if she wanted a room at the morgue, no strings attached, just some help on forensic cases for which he would, of course, pay her. Maggie jumped at the offer, and for more than a decade they had fallen into a friendly routine. He had never gotten married. Neither had she.

Maggie was startled by the awareness of someone in her room. She was relieved to see that it was Dan. He must have been standing there for a while, though she hadn't noticed when he entered. She was still a little groggy.

"Hi, Maggie."

"Hi, you big lug. Who do you think you are, holding me captive?"

"Got to get your attention somehow." With an awkward attempt to bow, he brought his right hand from behind his back with a flourish and produced a bouquet of flowers, a silly grin spreading across his face. Maggie's look of surprise was just what he needed. "Aha. Got your full attention now. I knew flowers would do it."

"Yes, you do, for about ten seconds," she said, though, inwardly, she was pleased at the gesture. "What do you think you're doing, taking my clothes and saying I can't go home? You want me to walk out of here buck naked? It can certainly be arranged."

"That I wouldn't mind seeing, Maggie, but it's also good to see that you are obviously on the road to recovery."

Maggie turned serious. "Dan, I have a problem." He moved closer to the bed and stared down at her, genuine concern in his eyes.

"What is it, Maggie?"

"It's Sidney."

"What do you mean?"

"He saw me, Dan. In the old days. At the White Swan. He knows I was Spider Rose." Dan smiled at the mention of Maggie's old stage name that, just between the two of them, he had called her nickname over the years.

"Oh, Maggie, that was a lifetime ago. That doesn't matter now. Everyone in New Orleans has a past."

"Perhaps, but what if he tells someone? It's Rodney Durham I'm thinking about. He's always looking for dirt. He probably would kill for this kind of dirt on me. You know that. Then he would drag you in. What about

162

your reelection? This could ruin you and me. Coroner and forensic anthropologist, strange bedfellows, literally. Your reputation would be suspect; mine would be ruined. Being a man, you probably would gain a certain new kind of respect, but women are never forgiven their pasts."

"Don't even think about it, Maggie. Everyone knows Sidney is a little nuts. He'll be transferred to an institution for the criminally insane. All of his ranting will mean nothing."

"But what if they do believe him, especially Rodney? You know his documentaries. Some of them border on slander. He could care less who he slams. In fact, I'm not so sure he doesn't already know about me. He gives me funny looks when he's around me. I want to slap the smile off his pimply face."

"Listen, Maggie, Rodney Durham won't be writing anything any time soon. He has problems of his own. Besides, don't you know that as long as Jimmy and Lucas and I are alive, no one can hurt you? It just won't happen."

For some crazy reason, Maggie believed him. She began to relax for the first time in days and felt herself drifting off to sleep, nothing on her mind but food, animals, and water. She dreamed about pots full of flowers that turned into shrimp po'boys when she watered them, and which tasted remarkably like her mother's lye soap.

Maggie awoke early the next day, ravenous and ready to go back to work. The staff had not needed to restrain her after all. A nurse's assistant brought a breakfast tray and the *Times-Picayune*.

Dan had been right. Rodney had problems of his

own. The headline read, "Local Documentary Producer Implicated in Hotel Bathtub Deaths." Maggie started reading the article. "Accused of callous indifference for human life, Rodney Durham, a local documentary producer, has been arrested for his alleged role in the deaths of two women in a recent hotel fire. . . ."

Maggie stopped reading the article. Then Jimmy O'Malley's name jumped out at her from under another headline: "Venetian Prostitutes Get Five Hundred Years Plus Eternity." She laughed out loud. Old and New Worlds collided again. Obviously, life in the Big Easy had begun to settle back into its normal routine. "Guess I'll be hearing from Italy sooner than expected."

Coming in 2013

If you enjoyed *Floating Souls*, look for
Mary Manhein's next novel,

Murder in the Cities of the Dead

....where murder, greed, the Catholic Church,
and voodoo all collide with
Maggie Andrepont,
Orleans Parish Forensic Anthropologist,
in New Orleans' infamous cemeteries,
the cities of the dead

RESEARCH · WRITING · PUBLISHING

Margaret Media, Inc. publishes Louisiana authors and topics exclusively. For more information visit: www.margaretmedia.com.

Women and New Orleans (1988) by Mary Gehman

The Free People of Color of New Orleans (1994) by Mary Gehman

Gumbo People (1999) by Dr. Sybil Kein

Touring Louisiana's Great River Road (2003) by Mary Gehman

Down at the End of the River (2008) by Angus Woodward

Marietta's House: A Grandmother's Cottage (2008) by J.E. Bourgoyne and J.G. Tyburski

Matters of the Heart: A Creole Love Story (2008) by Mary M. Culver

New Orleans Goes to the Movies: Film Sites in the French Quarter and Beyond (2008) by Alan Leonhard

My Name Is New Orleans: 40 Years of Poetry and Other Jazz (2009) by Arthur Pfister

A History of Pointe Coupée Parish, Louisiana (2010) by Brian J. Costello

Art Blakey Cookin' and Jammin': Recipes and Remembrances from a Jazz Life (2010) By Sandra Warren

New Orleans Besieged (2011) by D.K. Midkiff

War of the Pews: A Personal Account of St. Augustine Church in New Orleans (2011) by Rev. Jerome G. LeDoux, S.V.D.

Humanus Diabolicus: A Postmodern Prophecy (2012) by James Houk, PhD